SYSTEMA PARADOXA

ACCOUNTS OF CRYTOZOOLOGICAL IMPORT

VOLUME 02

GONE TO GROUND

A TALE OF THE WUNK

AS ACCOUNTED BY AARON ROSENBERG

NEOPARADOXA

Pennsville, NJ

2021

PUBLISHED BY
NeoParadoxa
A division of eSpec Books
PO Box 242
Pennsville, NJ 08070
www.especbooks.com

ISBN: 978-1-949691-53-5
ISBN (ebook): 978-1-949691-52-8

Interior Design: Danielle McPhail
www.sidhenadaire.com

Cover Art: Jason Whitley
Cover Design: Mike and Danielle McPhail, McP Digital Graphics
Interior Illustration: Jason Whitley

Copyediting: Greg Schauer

DEDICATION

For Dave Galanter
(1969-2020)
A dear friend gone much too soon

CHAPTER ONE

Everyone always agreed that, whatever else you might say about him, Trevor Kinkaid threw an excellent party. His house was of the larger variety, being done in the old style with high, vaulted ceilings, handsome inlaid floors, and a wide, sweeping staircase. It sat by the edge of the woods on one side and the sea on the other, thus taking advantage of both soothing sea air and welcoming shade. There were always plenty of spare bedrooms for those who imbibed too heavily and needed to be put up for the night. It was also a mark of distinction that it was even possible to imbibe, for Trevor was one of those who did not hold with Prohibition. He had no compunctions about acquiring whiskey and other potables from Canada and then making them freely available to his friends, or at least to those who chose to accept his frequent weekend invitations. He also stocked a good deal of food and nonalcoholic beverages, all of it of the highest quality, and as a result, his parties were the highlight of the season, and everyone made a point to attend.

This particular evening was no exception. The house was nearly full of people, or at least there were some in every room, so that while one could certainly still move around freely, it was also a bit of a challenge to find more than a moment of privacy. The women, mostly young and pretty, wore the latest fashions, with fringes and beads aplenty. Fascinators and feathers bobbed in time to their conversation, while cigarette holders dangled from their gloved fingers as they gestured. Their other hands cradled martini glasses, which they occasionally raised to brightly painted lips, hints of jasmine and rose and sandalwood and vanilla drifting about them. The men were either young and dashing or older and distinguished, dressed smartly in ascots and brightly polished shoes. Pipes or cigars outnumbered cigarettes, while martini glasses were as   prevalent as heavy cut-glass tumblers. Laughter and conversation rose everywhere, while music played from radios and record players, a different tune in every space but somehow not at all discordant, as if all the songs together melded into a single larger melody like flowers in a bouquet forming a harmonious whole.

Always the gracious host, Trevor drifted from room to room, carrying his habitual coffee mug rather than any actual glassware, pipe clamped firmly between his teeth, perhaps a touch paunchy now, his hair beginning to thin from its former thick waves, but his whiskers still neatly trimmed, his jaw still mostly firm, still a striking presence in his traditional red velvet smoking jacket. He knew most of his guests by name and always stopped to speak to each one, inquiring after their health, their recent pastimes — most of his guests were not so gauche as to have anything like an actual job! — their travels, and so forth before moving on with a smile and an encouragement to avail themselves fully of his hospitality.

It did not go unnoticed, of course, that for many of these perambulations, Trevor was not unaccompanied. This was nothing new, for he was still a handsome man and a charming one, if a trifle overbearing, and possessed of a fortune well in keeping with his grand home. Women were always eager to win his attention, and Trevor himself was more than happy to grant them such notice, for as long as it — and they — continued to amuse him.

At most parties, however, he played more of the gadfly, moving from lady to lady as easily as he went from room to room. Thus, the fact that one particular lady wandered with him for much of this evening drew some attention and a good deal of gossip. All of which seemed to entertain Trevor himself, while the lady appeared alternately flustered and determined to act as if oblivious to the whispers that trailed behind her like ribbons fluttering on the breeze.

Her name, it was gathered, was Lisette Barnes. She was from somewhere in the region, which is to say New England, and her manner and posture spoke of good breeding even if her robin's egg-hued dress was only barely still in fashion, her scent more clean soap than expensive perfume, and her beads of polished stone rather than pearl. Still, she was striking with her bright blue eyes, pert nose, petaled lips, and feathered blonde hair, and she did appear to enjoy Trevor's attentions, although there were those who wondered after they had disappeared from view whether indeed the pair were walking together or whether Lisette preceded their host, much like a scout before a patrol — or a lamb fleeing a wolf.

Still, no one heard her say a word to rebuff his advances, nor did anyone think that Trevor could be anything but gracious, even in defeat. Thus, when the couple failed to turn up in the next room after a time, those whose presence they had just vacated smirked amongst themselves, giggling and whispering and glancing furtively toward the upstairs, in the direction of Trevor's grand master bedroom.

When Trevor did reappear, however, it was not by descending the stairs, nor did he look triumphant. Indeed, he wandered into the sitting room in something of a daze, his face red and beaded with sweat, mud spattering his trouser cuffs. He went straight to the sideboard and poured himself a stiff drink, adding it directly to his mug and downing the lot in a single go.

Of the young lady, there was no sign.

After a few moments, he seemed to collect himself again and began to glance around, smiling and engaging in small talk with those guests nearby, his voice slowly returning to its customary volume and cheer, the furrows in his brow and by his eyes steadily easing.

He was his usual self again, all geniality and consideration, by the time they heard the screams.

CHAPTER TWO

"Good lord!" That was from James Winthrop—"Jimmy" to his friend, of whom there were many, at least as long as he was buying the drinks—who had been lounging against the bar trading idle quips with Trevor and a few others and who now bolted upright as if he'd been shot. "What, has someone spilled their drink?"

Everyone rose to their feet, casting about to see where the sounds had originated, and it was soon determined that they arose from out of doors. That quelled the curiosity of at least half, particularly among the women who did not want to risk ruining their heels or twisting their ankles on the dew-laden lawn, but most of the men and the more adventurous ladies rushed for the French doors, stepping to the edge of the wide patio and gazing out across the grass, trying to track the screams that continued to linger in the air.

"Over there!" Daniel Halsey declared, pointing, for even though one of Trevor's generation, his eyes were still sharp as a hawk's, particularly when a young lady might be involved. One liver-spotted hand, well-tanned from hours on the courts, gestured across the expansive lawn to where neatly trimmed grass gave way to untamed wildflowers and then brambles and ivy and leaves beneath the trees that encircled like an advancing horde. Squinting, the other guests could make out what Halsey had seen—a figure beneath those branches, stretched out upon the ground, a splash of pale blue that stood out against the green.

At once, several of the group started across the yard, heedless of the water seeping into shoes and socks and pants legs. Trevor was among them, though he was far from in the lead, and his motions could be said to be more reluctant than eager, as if he were being drawn toward the spectacle despite himself.

As perhaps the fittest among them—to the constant admiration of the women and the consternation of the other men—it was little surprise that Will Lowder should be the first to reach the site, using legs honed by many laps in the club pool. "Why, it's Lisette, isn't it?" he called, dropping to a crouch beside the figure. "But—oh, dear! I believe she may be—"

"Dead!" Halsey agreed, arriving at the scene and sinking to his knees as much from being out of breath as for a desire to examine the body. And examine her he did, and none there could gainsay his expert opinion, for before retiring he had run a highly successful medical practice. "She's definitely dead."

"Dead?" All eyes then turned from the fair Lisette to gaze at their host, who came to a stumbling halt still several paces from his companion of earlier. He stared at her with something akin to fright, but was it fear of death, fear of her, or fear of discovery that made him start so? Perhaps it was simply the heat of those many gazes, which were now far warmer than mere admiration could account for.

"Oh, she's dead, all right," Halsey repeated, reaching out with a callused hand to turn her head from side to side, his touch surprisingly gentle. "And from nothing so simple as a bee sting or a chicken bone. See here?" He indicated her slender neck, where fair skin already began to mottle, the dark hues blending in with the shade but standing out against her complexion. "Fingers did that. She's been strangled."

"Strangled?" It was the second time Trevor had repeated his old friend's statement, and if anything, the glares directed his way grew even sharper. Noticing this, he shook himself and straightened. "How horrible!" he declared, glaring right back at the assemblage, who had so recently hung upon his every word. "And at my party!"

"You were the last one to see her alive, were you not?" another guest, Pat Mercer, inquired, his tone as sharp as his chin, with which one could have shaved. Mercer fancied his wit to be as sharp as his features, and often claimed that he could have excelled at the practice of law if he'd only felt it to be worth his time.

"And your pants are wet!" Jimmy was quick to chime in. Such a statement might have drawn chuckles and sly comments normally, but now the admonition brought frowns and accusatory looks instead.

"I saw her," Trevor agreed huffily. "Of course. But I was not the last. No. That'd be whoever did this to her, no doubt." He gestured down at the dead girl, whose staring eyes Halsey had just closed.

"And who might that be?" Mercer demanded, stroking his chin with long, slender fingers. One could almost see the courtroom forming around him in his mind.

"I don't know," their host admitted. "I saw her out here, but from a distance. She was talking to someone, and it looked... heated. I didn't get involved—none of my affair, clearly." The look he cast toward her body was at least tinged with regret, though that seemed heavily leavened by irritation, even outrage. "Evidently, it did not turn out well for her."

A few of the others, having heard their host and friend's denial of culpability, turned away, apparently satisfied. But Mercer was not so easily relieved of the bone he had chosen to gnaw upon. "So you say you saw someone arguing with her," he restated. "Who was it? One of us?" And he gestured around him as if inviting the older man to cast blame elsewhere.

But Trevor shook his head.

"I don't know," he said slowly. "I wasn't close enough to make out a face." Then he brightened. "There was someone else, though! Someone out here in the woods! They must have seen!"

That sent a murmur through the crowd. A witness would certainly be able to confirm Trevor's innocence. "Who was it?" Halsey asked, clearly eager to believe his old friend. "Who else was out here?"

They all turned to stare at Trevor, only to frown as he sagged. "I'm not sure," came the eventual reply, as if dragged from his reluctant lips. "I couldn't see. Just that there was someone here—their face stood out against the leaves and branches."

"So," Mercer dragged the word out, tapping his cheek with a forefinger. "You admit to seeing her out here but claim she was with someone else—someone you couldn't see to identify. And you say there was someone else who might have seen this as well, a witness—but you can't name them, either? How convenient."

Trevor bristled and took a step toward the younger man, who had the good sense to drop his posturing and back up a pace. But several of the others interposed themselves. "We'd best notify the authorities," Halsey advised. "They can take it from here."

Though he did not like the idea of ceding any control over his domain, even in such dire circumstances, Trevor clearly saw the logic in this, for he nodded once, brusquely. "Indeed, let's get them down here," he agreed, turning back toward the house. "The sooner they can settle this matter, the better."

"What about her?" Will asked as the others all began their retreat. He was still beside poor dead Lisette, and looked as if he might cry, his own fair features flushed. "We can't just leave her here like this, can we?" For all his physical prowess, Will was a sensitive young man, which many of the ladies in their set only found even more appealing.

"There's nothing to be done for her at the moment," Halsey stated, but paused. "Still, someone should keep an eye out, make sure she is not meddled with."

"I'll stay," Will offered at once, and everyone nodded. There was little question of his having an ulterior motive or a sinister aim, for both would have required more thought than he was believed capable of mustering. Indeed, many in their circle likened Will to a fine retriever, all handsome and golden and friendly but without a great deal of intellect. Still, there were far worse traits to be had, and at least he would make an excellent guardian for the recently deceased damsel. Thus the others were content to leave him behind, there at the edge of the woods, as they returned to the house and made for the phone to call in the police.

Those who had remained at the house were eager to hear what had occurred, of course. There was some initial concern over whether drinks should be concealed or poured out, given that the arrival of police on the scene might be imminent, but it was widely held that the officials would overlook even flagrant flaunting of Prohibition, given the circumstances. Besides which, everyone was far more interested in discussing Lisette and her fate. In particular, women like Bridget and Daphne voraciously sought any and all details, the one because she lived to know and critique and the other because she had a vested interest in her surroundings. By the time the phone call had been made, the entire house was abuzz with the news—and Trevor found himself being eyed in a very different manner than that to which he was accustomed, which was very much not to his liking.

CHAPTER THREE

It was a mark of Trevor's importance in the community — or perhaps the quiet of the day — that it took the police so little time to arrive that many of the female guests were still in the process of changing outfits. Thus it was that the crowd gathering around for a look down the stairs and from the surrounding rooms was smaller than it might have been as Trevor, now fully restored to himself, answered the sharp rap on the door.

"Mr. Kinkaid?" The man asking was nearly Trevor's height, but of a leaner build, mild features offset by sharp, dark eyes, his suit unfashionably of an equally dark hue and his shirt a bland, standard white, but at least his hat showed some quality, being a felt fedora that shaded his face and cast strong shadows across his clean cheeks and jaw. "Detective Allan Davis. I understand there's been an incident." Davis showed his credentials, after which Trevor stepped back and allowed him to enter, though grudgingly. While he was still lord of the manor, it was difficult to escape the bare fact that he was ceding much of his control to this unstylish newcomer.

Still, current need outweighed his pride, and he nodded. "Yes. This way." He led Davis and the men who followed him in — three in uniform, two without — through the house, drawing a crowd as they went. Another officer declined to enter, stationing himself instead just outside the front door. "It's — she's — out back," he explained as he strode through, acknowledging the onlookers with only a curt nod.

"Thank you." Though there were clear signs of drinking all about and a veritable haze of alcohol in the air, the police did not pause in their progress, nor remark upon the fumes and bottles present. At the French doors, however, the inspector finally stopped and turned to look pointedly at Trevor's guests. He did not say a word, but his sharp gaze was enough and they all fell back, staying politely within as he and his officers followed Trevor outside without any other accompaniment.

They did not run, and so it seemed to take a good deal longer to cross that fine lawn than it had before, at least to Trevor's mind. The woods felt miles away, and though the sun was beginning to wend its way toward the horizon, he was still sweating by the time they neared the body, and its faithful warden.

Will had straightened almost to attention when he'd spotted the approaching men, looking like nothing so much as a little boy playing at soldier. He easily picked Davis out as the man in charge, and it was to the inspector that he directed his statement of, "No one has come near, sir, nor disturbed her rest." One of the two men not in uniform had fallen behind on the approach, but the other quickly produced a large camera with an equally impressive flash and began photographing the scene and its surroundings.

"Thank you," Davis told him gravely, offering a hand, which Will shook gladly and with some gratitude for the recognition. "And you are?"

"Oh! Will Lowder, sir. William. William J. The J is for James. I was with them when they found her, and I offered to stay here and make sure no one bothered her." The words came out all in a rush, and the young man kept his eyes fixed on the detective the whole time, assiduously avoiding the sight of that unfortunate young woman. He had been much the same as they'd neared, Davis had noted, standing guard but either afraid to look upon the dead or averting his gaze out of respect. Either way, the young man seemed earnest and eager to please.

"When you say 'they found her,'" was Davis's next question, directed at both the guardian and his host, "who do you mean, exactly? Who was here when the body was discovered?"

"Hm," Will began, frowning as he did his best to recollect, but Trevor interrupted.

"It was the two of us," he answered concisely, "plus Daniel Halsey, Jimmy Winthrop, Larry Todd, and Pat Mercer." That last name said with a dismissive sneer. "There were others who followed us from the sitting room, but we were the only ones who actually crossed the lawn fully. The rest petered out along the way."

Davis had produced a small notebook from his jacket pocket, and a pen—one of those new plastic types, a surprisingly vibrant blue instead of the more traditional black—and quickly jotted down the names. "And when was this, more or less?"

"Perhaps an hour ago?" Trevor estimated. But this time, it was his young guest who showed him up, not the other way round.

"It was half-past three," Will stated decisively. "I remember because we were all inside and Bridget had just remarked how it was nearly time to dress for cocktails."

"Half-past three. Thank you." Davis made a note of that, then checked his wristwatch—a solid, utilitarian timepiece, the other men noted. "And it's just four fifteen now. You wasted no time calling us." That last was said with complete neutrality, neither accusing nor praising, yet Trevor bristled nonetheless.

"Of course, I didn't!" he stated, practically sputtering with indignation. "A young lady dead, and at my house, in the midst of my party! I called you at once! It's a tragedy and an outrage!" It was clear from his manner and his red face which of the two were affecting him more, though his gaze did slip to the late Miss Barnes with something approaching regret and perhaps even tenderness.

Checking the ground around him first, Davis knelt carefully by the young woman's side. "Carruthers, go help the doc," he instructed over his shoulder, and one of the officers nodded and hurriedly retraced his steps back toward the house. "Do you know who she is?" he asked, his alert gaze taking in the details of her features, clothing, and posture before coming to rest upon her neck, where the marks were now vivid and garish against her pale skin.

"Lisette Barnes," Trevor ground out, his jaw clenched and the muscles along it jumping. "I'd not met her before today."

Will opened his mouth, about to speak, but a glare from his host stopped him before any sound emerged. Davis noticed the sharp intake of breath, however, and looked up, one eyebrow rising. "Something to add?" he inquired, his tone mild but the message behind it unmistakable. This was not a request.

"It's just..." The young man had the good grace to look away, studying his own hands, which were strong and slightly chapped. "For a first-timer, she sure got a lot of your attention."

That produced another momentary sputter from Trevor, but now Davis's gaze had swung to him, and the host felt equally compelled to answer honestly. "Well, yes, I was intrigued, even captivated. I mean, look at her!" He gestured toward Lisette, though without looking her way. "She was lovely, and fresh, and far less... complicated... than most of the women in our set. I found her engaging and her honest pleasure at the party refreshing."

The detective rose to his feet, brushing any hint of grass or dirt from his knees as he did. "So it would be fair to say that you spent a good deal of time with her before her death?"

Trevor frowned and jutted out his jaw but could not deny something so easily checked with anyone present. "I did."

"And was the young lady... amenable to your attentions?" Delicately worded, especially for a policeman, but still Trevor took offense, puffing up in an attempt to loom over the other man.

"I would never force my attentions on a woman!" he all but roared. "Miss Barnes was charming company, and we were having a lovely afternoon, all perfectly polite and respectable!"

Davis nodded as if that had been all but assumed, though he immediately followed up with, "And when was the last time you saw her? Before—" his gesture took in the dead woman and her surroundings, and could have been taken to mean "before her death" or "before you found her here" or even "before you did this to her." It was a masterful display of encompassing many possibilities at once, laying the cards out on the table so that Trevor would be forced to select one himself and thus demonstrate something by his choice.

"I couldn't say, precisely," was the answer, as carefully worded as a court testimony, the older man's thoughts almost visible as they churned through possible responses for the least objectionable—and the least implicating. "We parted company—amicably!—after a time. I went on to another room and other guests, and I don't know where she went. I didn't see her again until I happened outside and spotted her all the way over here." He spoke slowly, carefully, making sure each word was heard and understood. "She was with someone. They looked to be arguing. They were too far away for me to see who it was—I knew her mostly by the color of her dress. I spotted someone else nearby, too. In the woods, just there." He pointed. "It seemed a personal affair, so I gave them their privacy and turned back toward the house."

"Do you know approximately what time that might have been?"

"Around three, perhaps?" Trevor shook his head. "I'm sorry, I wasn't looking at the time." He attempted a smile, though it faltered away a second later. "My parties tend to pass in a bit of a whirl."

Just then, Carruthers returned, assisting another man in crossing the damp ground. This gentleman was older, more of Trevor's own generation, and shorter, heavier, with thick bushy dark hair and a suit of a handsome plaid pattern but an unfortunate green shade. The black leather bag clutched in his arms announced his profession to the world, and with a single nod from Davis, he crouched by the deceased, setting the bag beside him and unlatching it to first pull on heavy rubber gloves and then draw forth a magnifying lens.

"Hm, dead perhaps two hours," the doctor—for so he was, Doctor Peterson by name—declared after a moment, having tugged up one glove to check body temperature against the back of his hand and then studied the way her head moved and her arm fell when he shifted each in turn. "By strangulation, clearly." He tapped the marks as he said this. "I can tell more once I do a full exam, but I expect those two details will be proven easily enough." He frowned as he straightened to his full height again. "Unfortunate, with this trend toward ladies wearing gloves—no real chance of defensive marks. I can't tell if she put up a struggle. Right now, I'm not seeing fingerprints on her, either, though I'll know for sure once I have her on the table." He cocked his head to one side, waiting for the inspector to reply.

Davis took only a moment to nod. "Be careful lifting her," he warned—unnecessarily, judging by the doctor's offended expression. "The ground's been a bit trampled here"—Will looked away guiltily at that quiet reprimand, while Trevor merely *harrumph*ed under his breath—"but we still may be able to draw some conclusions from the scene."

The doctor nodded and bustled away, presumably to summon assistants who would then carry the young lady off to the city morgue. The photographer, having finished his own task, departed as well, back to the station to develop his film. Davis watched them go before returning his attention to the two men beside him.

"I'm afraid I'll have to make a bit of a nuisance of myself," he warned Trevor, only the barest hint of a smile playing across his thin lips to indicate that this was meant as something akin to a joke. "I'll need to question everyone here. No one leaves until we're done— I'll radio back for more men, and I'll be posting some at each door once they've arrived. I trust I can expect your full cooperation?" Again, this was not a question. It was impressive how a man of such unremarkable features could take on such unshakable authority when imbued with the weight of the law.

Nor was Trevor slow to respond or to acknowledge the shift in power. "Of course," he asserted at once. "Anything I can do to help. We all want whoever did this dealt with as quickly as possible." The implication in that statement was obvious, but the detective let it slide off him, only granting the older man a firm nod of thanks for his support. Clearly, the investigation would be conducted with all thoroughness and impartiality, and whoever the culprit was, they would be held accountable for their actions. Regardless of wealth or position.

"Excellent," Davis stated. "I'll leave a man or two here to keep the site secure. Meanwhile, I'll need a room to work from, if you don't mind. Somewhere I can interview your guests in private." That smile flickered past once more. "I'll try not to disrupt the party too much." He gave the homeowner a pointed glance and stated, slowly and clearly, so there could be no misunderstanding, "My only concern here is the young lady's death."

There was nothing to be given to that beyond silent acquiescence and a brief nod of appreciation for the detective's obvious discretion, and so Trevor simply turned and led the way back to the house, the detective stepping to one side of him, Will to the other. One of the officers trailed after them, while Carruthers and an officer named Grant remained behind to stand vigil over the fallen in her sky-blue raiment. There was little more that could be done for her just now, but perhaps she would rest easier knowing that the wheels of justice had begun to turn on her behalf.

CHAPTER FOUR

The detective reentered the house like the prow of a ship, his focus slicing through the still, slightly churning waters of Trevor's guests—though it was obvious all of them were dying to know details, they parted without a single question, gliding aside so that he could stride through them, passing down the narrow alleyway bordered by their intense interest without ever being impinged upon by it. Trevor did his best to get out in front of the wave but was unable to match Davis's pace or concentration. The host finally resorted to laying a hand on the younger man's arm, which caused him to stop at once.

"I believe the den will serve your purposes best," Trevor explained, gesturing toward a set of handsome pocket doors just to their right. Davis nodded and followed as he slid the doors apart, revealing a classically appointed study complete with floor-to-ceiling bookcases, a large leather-topped desk, and well-stuffed leather armchairs and couch. The tall windows along the outer wall looked out on the lawn, and from here, Davis could easily see Carruthers and the second officer, Grant, relaxed but on guard over the body of Lisette Barnes.

"Yes, this will do nicely, thank you," Davis agreed, stepping over to the broad, handsome desk. He slid the chair out and sank into it, allowing himself a second to appreciate the soft leather before returning to his usual upright posture. "Would you mind?" he asked, gesturing at one of the two armchairs and displaying again that impressive ability to frame a directive as a polite question.

Trevor nodded and took a seat, perching on the edge of the chair like a schoolboy waiting to be scolded. "More questions?" He looked displeased but resigned to that prospect even before the detective nodded.

"It's just this," Davis began, leaning forward, both forearms on the desktop before him. "I will, as I said, be questioning everyone here. And I expect I'll get conflicting reports, of course—that's bound to happen when you have a large number of people about. Everyone sees things through their own biases. But I have a great deal of practice, so you can rest assured I'll eventually sort through everything, eliminate those idiosyncrasies, and piece together the truth." He fixed that sharp gaze of his upon his host. "Since that is the case, and as we are now alone here"—he had already set his other two officers to guard the front door and prevent any of the guests from leaving—"I wanted to give you the chance to amend your previous statements."

The older man bristled at that. "What do you mean? I've already told you, I didn't kill her!"

"You did say that, yes," Davis agreed. "You also said that you and Miss Barnes were friendly throughout the party, and that when you did part ways, it was amicably." His expression was carefully nonjudgmental. "You are, I daresay, a good deal older than she was, wouldn't you agree? You're a wealthy man, influential, plus it's your party. That puts you in a position of power. She was young, pretty, and new. I'm sure she was flattered by your interest, but I have to ask— and, again, it is just the two of us here, and I promise you only relevant details will be included in my report—whether it was all as pleasant and reciprocal as you've implied?"

For a moment, the two men merely looked at each other, the one glaring, the other carefully meeting his gaze but not rising to the attempt at confrontation. Predictably, it was Trevor who looked away first. "I didn't force myself upon her, if that's what you're asking," he grumbled. "I would never do such a thing. I don't care if it is my blasted party!" He glanced back up. "But it might be fair to say that I was... perhaps more interested in her than she in me."

Davis said nothing, did not move, merely waited, allowing the space for his host to continue.

"We were getting along famously," Trevor expounded after a second or two of silence. "She was bright and pretty and laughed at all my jokes. Can you blame me for thinking perhaps she was... attracted to me as well?" His cheeks flushed but, now that he'd begun, he continued doggedly, "I asked her if she'd care to accompany me upstairs. No beating around the bush for me, I see what I want and I go for it! Well"—he blew out a breath—"she didn't bother being evasive with her answer, either. Wasn't rude about it, was flattered and flustered, but said no, she didn't think that would be wise for either of us."

"And how did you take that?" Davis asked, his tone neither accusatory nor conciliatory.

"I might've gotten a bit hot under the collar," came the reply. "You're right, I'm not used to being turned down. And I really thought she was interested. So, yes, I was thrown off, even insulted. I told her off a bit. I mean, here she was, in my house, eating my food, drinking my..." he suddenly remembered who he was speaking to and, despite the promise to overlook such things, changed what he'd been about to say to "refreshments, walking with me, talking with me, laughing with me, and now she says she's not interested? Was it all just a big tease?" He frowned, though it seemed that expression might have been meant for himself rather than the unfortunate young lady. "I... was not my usual gentlemanly self. It's true. I was a wounded bear, and I lashed out." He met Davis' gaze once more. "But that was all. I told her if I wasn't good enough, maybe she should find someone who was, and I stormed off."

"And the next time you saw her?" The detective asked.

"Was outside," Trevor confirmed. "But not up close. I stomped around the house a bit, trying to cool down, but as you might've noticed, there's not a lot of privacy when I've got a party on, not unless I felt like heading upstairs, and that felt like too much work. So I went out onto the lawn instead. I saw her there, across the yard, just where we found her. She was with someone else, though I couldn't make out who. They looked to be arguing." He shook his head. "I admit, I took some pleasure in that—it almost felt as if she had taken me up on my suggestion and settled on someone else immediately, only now it wasn't going to her liking, and that felt like a just comeuppance. But whatever it was, I figured it was none of my business. She'd made her own bed, and I was determined to let her lie in it." He sighed. "Now it appears that was wholly the wrong decision, and thus the fault for her death is at least partly on me." He did not waver, however, as he added, "but I never approached her, and I most certainly did not harm her, much less kill her!"

Davis waited another moment, until it was clear his host had finished. "Thank you," he stated at last. "That does provide a clearer picture, and I suspect it will be very helpful in figuring out what did occur." He leaned back in the chair, letting his hands fall to the leather-covered arms. "I think I'll take a minute and then circulate a little, after which I'll see if I need to bring anyone in here for a more private conversation."

Though Trevor was not a man accustomed to being dismissed, in this instance, he seemed delighted to be and was up from his chair like a shot. "Of course, of course," he said, already stepping quickly toward the doors. "I'll leave you to it. Whatever you need, just say the word." He had just reached for the inset handles when the inspector called his name.

"The most important thing," Davis instructed when his host glanced back, "is to not prejudice others by revealing any details to them. Not about our conversation and not about what happened to Miss Barnes. If anyone asks you anything — and they will — just tell them they'll have to bring any questions straight to me."

Trevor nodded and let himself out, sliding the doors shut again behind him and leaving Davis alone in the expensive room with only tasteful furniture and thoughts of a dead woman for company.

Of course, it was not possible that word of Lisette's untimely death should be kept from the other guests. After all, even if Trevor had abided by the detective's wishes, he had hardly been alone when he had discovered her body, and the rest were not so constrained by either decorum or any fear of seeming guilty. Thus when he stepped back out of the study, the rest of the house was already abuzz about the poor young lady, and many had begun offering their own theories on exactly what had happened to her and who might be responsible. Many a questioning glance was sent Trevor's way, as he had been the victim's companion for much of the day and had just emerged from being questioned by the police. Still, such was his dignity and reputation that the whispers were still mostly kept behind his back, at least for now. Nor was the common opinion decided against him just yet, as people still wondered who else could have had cause to harm the young lady.

One of those asking questions was a woman of similar age to the victim. Indeed, the two appeared to have much in common, for this woman was also a newcomer to Trevor's parties and, although her features were not as fine as Lisette's, nor her hair as golden or her eyes as blue, still there was enough of a similar cast to their looks that many began to whisper that this young woman was, in fact, the late Lisette's sister. Certainly, it would explain her tenacity at asking what happened, for Winnie—that was the name she gave, in a voice soft enough one had to listen closely to hear it—seemed determined to get to the truth of what had happened, no matter what.

The other oddity about Winnie, besides her possible connection to Lisette and her soft voice and shy manner that were so different from most of the bold, brash, brightly colored young women of the set, was that her newness was even more pronounced than that of her supposed sister. After sitting with Jimmy and Bridget and a few of the others for a time in the drawing room, asking Jimmy exactly what he had seen and heard out by the woods, Winnie eventually excused herself and drifted away, presumably to question someone else. As soon as she was out of earshot, Bridget started in on her.

"What an odd little creature!" she commented, tapping her ivory cigarette holder against her cheek in a way that made the feathers atop her head bob and wave and produced a fresh burst of Habanita around her head. "Like a little mouse, but a mouse with a bone caught firmly in its jaws!"

The others laughed, for Bridget was the sort who always said such sharply funny things, and her description was entirely apt.

"You know what's odd, though?" Jimmy commented, patting Bridget's knee to apologize for cutting off whatever her next cutting remark might be. "I don't believe I've ever seen her here before. Have you?"

Everyone else shook their heads, and one of the other ladies, Monica, said, "Well, no, dear, you wouldn't have, would you? Today was Lisette's first time with us as well—and look how that turned out, the poor thing!" Monica was a few years older than her friends, though still well behind Trevor, and often took a maternal interest in their well-being.

"That's not exactly what I mean, though," Jimmy insisted. "Yes, this was Lisette's first party here, but she was around most of the day—we all saw her flitting from room to room, pretty as a songbird, with Trevor drooling along behind her." That got a laugh, and a glare from Bridget, who evidently wished she had been the one to make such a droll observation. "But this girl, Winnie, I don't recall seeing her with Lisette, or around at all before—well, before she sat down with us. Do you?"

It was a fair question, and a serious one, and Bridget was not so flighty she could not set her witticisms aside for genuine thought, which was why after a moment, she shook her head. "You know, I don't either," she agreed. "How odd... It's like she just appeared from nowhere." Then she laughed. "But surely that's just because she's so drab and quiet she blends into the woodwork? Especially in that dress — I mean, really? Dove gray? It's summer, darling!"

The others all chuckled at this latest dig, the women most of all, and their talk quickly moved to the latest fashions and the colors that were currently in vogue, like the champagne shade Bridget herself was boasting. Poor Winnie was forgotten, though perhaps that was a kinder fate than continuing to be a target for the others' humor.

CHAPTER FIVE

Pat Mercer was another who had decided not to leave the investigation strictly in the hands of the police. "I don't see that it's really any of their concern," he'd told as many as would listen with a sniff. "After all, they're hardly of our social circle, are they? Why should they care what happened to poor Lisette? And if they don't care, they'll do shoddy work—I've seen enough of that from waiters and tailors and other menials, doing only the bare minimum. Bad enough when it's only a question of the soup being cold or my collars not receiving enough starch, but this is a young woman's murder we're talking about! No," he'd insisted, straightening to his full height, an action that would have shown to greater effect if he'd had a few more inches on him. "If this is to be done properly, it must be investigated by one of our own. And I believe I am more than man enough for the task."

Thus it was that he had taken it upon himself to step back outside and approach the scene of the crime, where Carruthers and Grant stiffened as soon as they saw him marching toward them. "Can we help you, sir?" Carruthers asked politely but firmly, interposing himself when Mercer would have stepped around him. The doctor had already removed Lisette's body, and now only a faint depression in the grass and leaves indicated where her life had so recently ended.

"You can," Mercer replied sharply. "You can stand aside, there's a good man. I am here to see to the scene and determine exactly what happened. The sooner this crime is solved, the better for all of us." He had already been annoyed by Davis's other officers when he had attempted to go out to his car and retrieve a spare blazer he kept in the trunk for emergencies. The two policemen stationed at the front door had informed him, however, that there was to be no unauthorized movement in or out of the house as long as the investigation was ongoing. Mercer had strenuously objected, of course, nor had he been the first to do so, many of the other guests deciding the excitement of watching a murder investigation was far better appreciated from the comfort of one's own home, with the latest details shared by telephone, but to no avail—the officers had been civil but had refused to budge for anyone, including one Patrick Thomas Mercer the Third. So he was even more put out to find yet more uniforms blocking his path now.

And block his path they did. "We appreciate your desire to help, sir," Carruthers continued—he was by far the more adept at soothing ruffled feathers between himself and Grant. "But this is a police matter. I'll have to ask you to step away." With that, the officer did his best impression of a statue, lifting his chin to gaze out past Mercer with that implacable look that said, *"I am here and shall not be moved."*

Unfortunately, Mercer was even less accustomed to not getting his way than Trevor and far less skilled at handling such naked effrontery. "Now, see here," he started, taking another step forward and glaring up at Carruthers, their faces only inches apart. "Do you have any idea—?"

Anything further he might have said was rudely interrupted by a thick forearm, clad all in navy, shoving its way between the two men and forcing Mercer back two, three steps all in a rush. The arm belonged to Grant, who now shouldered his way in front of his partner and glared down at Mercer. This was not the dispassionate gaze of a statue, but rather the fierce glower of an aggressor, visibly hostile and barely contained, much like a ferocious dog straining to be let off its leash.

"We don't care who you are," he growled down at the shocked and bewildered Mercer. "You ain't police, you ain't getting near. Now back off, afore we arrest you for obstruction and haul you off to jail." Grant took a menacing step forward, and Mercer hurriedly retreated until there were several feet of open space between them. This was why Grant and Carruthers made such good partners, in addition to both being stalwart officers, alert and obedient and with a keen belief that their job was to make the world a safer and more peaceful place—Carruthers was the smooth-talker, the politician, whereas Grant was the enforcer who stepped in when diplomacy proved not enough.

"Well!" Was what Mercer finally came up with when he was able to formulate coherent speech again. He straightened his lapels and brushed imaginary dirt from his sleeves. "I believe I'll be contacting the Commissioner about such behavior!" Neither officer reacted to such an empty threat and, thus thwarted, the would-be investigator turned away—and then stopped as another thought occurred to him. "Where, exactly am I not allowed?" he asked carefully.

"Right here," Grant replied, waving a hand at the crime scene. "No civilians allowed."

"Yes, fine, understood." Mercer backed away, then angled to the right and walked slowly, carefully around the two men, not toward the spot they guarded but toward the woods beyond. For he had just remembered Trevor's story about there being another witness. Surely that would be equally important to proving—or discounting—his innocence? And if the police were too dull-witted to think of that, well then, Pat Mercer would just have to do their jobs for them!

Entering the woods was a novel experience for Mercer, whose closest experience with wildlife was usually admiring trees from a distance or, more frequently, lamenting their presence bordering his favorite golf course. Now here he was, stepping into the shade of a veritable forest, and he mentally congratulated himself on such fortitude and bravery, even as he tried not to shiver from being cut off from the last rays of sunlight. Every step made him cringe as leaves and pine needles crunched beneath his feet, and the rustling of leaves and branches made him jump and start. It was good that no one else was around beyond those two uniforms, and they had already returned their attention to watching for any approach from the house! He would hate to have anyone who mattered see him like this!

Still, Mercer consoled himself, it would not matter once he discovered the vital clue that settled this case. He would be the toast of the town—Pat Mercer, Esquire, who solved a murder singlehanded! Trevor would be in his debt, as well—unless, of course, he was the guilty party, in which case all his other potential victims would be undyingly grateful instead. Either way, what was a small amount of discomfort compared to that?

With those thoughts firmly in mind, Mercer steeled himself for the task at hand and ventured further into the woods, trying to ignore the way the trees seemed to close in around him and the way the air seemed to thicken, becoming murky and difficult to breathe. He remembered more or less where Trevor had pointed during his recounting and headed in that direction, trying to watch his footing—for one never knew what manner of creature might have been here, doing who knows what!—while also watching around him for low-hanging branches, loose vines, lurking jungle cats, and other dangers.

It was, then, perhaps surprising that he managed to find anything at all. But find something he did, and Carruthers and Grant were soon startled by a loud "Aha!" that emerged from the woods perhaps ten, twenty feet beyond their position. Their recent confronter appeared a moment later, leaping out of the trees as if to declaim upon a stage—or perhaps as if fleeing from some hidden menace. "You there!" he called out, pointing at Grant. "Run and tell your superior that I have found something here of vital importance!"

Grant growled at the demand and its imperious tone, then looked to Carruthers, who nodded after a moment. "Just in case it's something," his partner pointed out. "I'll keep an eye on things here." With that, Grant hurried toward the house and Davis. "And what've you found back there, sir?" Carruthers asked once it was just him and Mercer out there. "Not another body, I hope?"

"No, not another body, though I shouldn't be surprised, this gloomy forest could hide any number of them," Mercer snapped, but he was feeling far too triumphant to stay annoyed for very long. "Come see, then, if you must. Just take care not to disturb anything. Need to keep the scene pristine, don't you know."

"Of course, sir. I'll do my best." It was a mark of Carruthers' professionalism that he did allow even a hint of sarcasm to surface in his tone. He sidled over to where Mercer waited, turning carefully so that he could still keep the original crime scene in view as he went. "And what am I looking at, exactly?" he asked once he'd reached the other man.

"Right there, behind those bushes," Mercer stated, pointing to a particular clump of greenery. "That's where Trevor—Mister Kinkaid to you—said he saw someone. Someone who would've been in a position to see what really happened and who did it."

Now Carruthers was all business. "And you've found signs of that witness?" he asked, just as Davis arrived at a near-run, slightly out of breath from his quick pace.

"I did indeed." Mercer's answer was addressed to this larger audience of three, Grant having returned as well. "Although"—and here his confidence faltered slightly—"I am not sure I understand it entirely."

"Show me," Davis ordered, taking charge at once, and such was his quiet authority that Mercer did so without complaint, edging his way back into the woods with only the mildest shudder and leading the rest to a particular spot. "Here," he said, pointing at the ground before him. "You see it, don't you?"

The detective had already dropped to his knees, unheeding of the way dirt stained his trouser legs. "I see it," he confirmed, staring at the prints there. They were clearly footprints, though the ground here was both so littered with old leaves and so soft that the marks were not distinct enough to tell much beyond the fact that they had definitely been left by a person, and one wearing shoes.

The other problem, however, and the reason Mercer had hesitated, was because there were three, no four clear sets of the prints — and then nothing. They simply stopped. The ground was no different there — if anything, it was cleaner, with less debris — but it was also visibly undisturbed.

Davis quickly combed the area, Carruthers doing the same. Grant had returned to the murder scene without having to be told. Between them, while Mercer simply stood uncomprehending in their midst, the two policemen examined their surroundings, but to no avail. There were no other prints to be found. It was as if whoever had stood there had simply vanished into thin air.

Possibly taking Trevor's only alibi with them.

CHAPTER SIX

Back inside, Mercer wasted no time in telling everyone within hearing range exactly what he had found — with a clear emphasis on the fact that *he* was the one who had found it. What might have been a mere two-minute recitation of the facts instead became a twenty-minute diatribe on the incompetency of the police, the inadequacy of people below a certain social class, and the sterling qualities Mercer himself — and, by extension, the rest of the guests — had displayed in direct contradiction to those of Davis and his uniformed thugs.

There were several highly satisfactory *oohs* and *aahs* from his audience throughout all this — but not everyone was equally impressed by the young man's investigatory prowess and mental acuity. "Didn't you just say that you lost the footprints after only a few paces?" Bridget inquired, taking a sip from the martini one of her many admirers had fetched her. "That hardly seems like sterling detective work, dear. A bit shoddy, in fact, if you ask me — 'oh, here's a clue — no, wait, I've lost it again.'" That produced many a titter around the room, and Mercer froze mid-self-congratulation to glare down at her, a feat only possible because she was seated and he was not.

"At least I found the tracks in the first place!" he snapped. "That's more than those idiots in blue could do! And they do disappear! I didn't lose them, they just aren't there!"

Bridget blinked lazily at him, showing her smoky eye to good effect. "So, what," she drawled out over the lip of her glass, "this mysterious witness just leapt up into the trees after those few steps? Or perhaps he flew away? Ah, it could be that a giant bird dove down and swooped him up — upon command, of course!"

The titters had evolved into full-blown laughter, much of it at Mercer's expense, and he blinked, unsure how he had so suddenly lost the support of the room but aware that every second made it harder for him to win it back. He was about to offer some clever rejoinder that was sure to finally put Bridget in her place once and for all and firmly establish him as the premier mind and wit in the room—and, indeed, at the party and even in the wider circle of their mutual acquaintances—when another voice rose from a far corner and cut him off.

"No no no," the speaker offered, rising slowly from the armchair in which she had been lounging, her own empty cup dangling dangerously from slender fingers, ebon cigarette holder twirling between the fingers of the other hand, fascinator bouncing forward so far as to nearly drape into her eyes, her ascent trailed by the distinctive notes of jasmine and rose that shouted Chanel. "It's obvious what actually happened here. Your witness is a Wunk!"

Everyone turned and stared, which at least took the pressure off young Mercer. Sylvia Beaumont was an established feature at these soirees, in much the same way that a rather hideous bust in one of the antechambers might be—fascinating, a bit off-putting, not something most people would include but something that simply could not be removed or even fully ignored. Her late husband Mitchell had been one of Trevor's closest friends, after all, and so Sylvia was always included on his guest lists as a matter of course. She was one of the few who had known him long enough and well enough to speak her mind without fear of repercussion, and she often did so, to the occasional delight of the younger set who marveled at her daring and her brash nature. Bridget, in particular, seemed to admire the older woman and could often be found sitting with Sylvia, providing the latest gossip in exchange for old sordid details most had long since forgotten.

What prevented Sylvia from being as wildly popular as her young protégé were two things. The first was that she drank steadily and excessively, usually starting each party fully lucid and with a biting wit but progressing slowly and inevitably into near-somnambulance, becoming a fixture in physical truth as well as a metaphorical one, sinking into immobility in the armchair she had claimed more than a decade ago and stirring only to blink blearily at her surroundings from time to time or to accost someone into bringing her a fresh drink. The fact that she was on her feet now, and speaking, was enough of a rarity to attract attention and no small amount of wonder.

The other reason many of the younger crowd avoided her was because it was widely held that she had, in fact, lost any rhyme or reason and often spouted utter nonsense.

That appeared to be the case now, though Bridget valiantly sought to defend her mentor by asking, "And who, pray tell, is a Wunk when he's at home?" but without any of her usual acidity.

"Not a who at all," Sylvia replied, turning a surprisingly clear gaze upon her young friend, despite the drooping feathers nearly obscuring her sight. "But a what. A Wunk is not a person, it is a creature, a fixture of local legend."

Bridget frowned, for there was a fresh wave of tittering, and for once, she was not its instigator. "Well then, my dear, by all means, tell us about this Wunk," she entreated, raising her glass in silent toast to her mentor, or perhaps an equally silent request that the answer should prove to be elucidating but also not as far-fetched as it began to seem it might.

"A Wunk," Sylvia declaimed, and for all her age and frailty and inebriation her voice rang out clear and true, filling the large room, "is a creature that can only be found here in New England. It was first discovered by lumberjacks and has been spoken of ever since. They are exceedingly rare, however, and so it is no surprise that you would not have heard of them."

"What do they look like, these Wunks?" Winthrop asked, and where Bridget's voice had been devoid of venom, his was filled to the brim. There were those among the party set who sometimes murmured about the evident rivalry between those two young wits, wondering if there had perhaps been a time when they had been intimates and had somehow fallen out, and it was not uncommon for them to compete — or for Winthrop to needle Bridget by making unpleasant and not always wholly inaccurate comments about the state, sobriety, and sanity of her chosen mentor. Now appeared to be one of those times. "And how," he continued, "could some... creature... have been the creator of Pat's elusive footprints? Is this a case of a bear learning to wear shoes?" Several people laughed at that, though they were quickly shushed, for the room was now aquiver with tension, and everyone wanted to see how it would break and whom it would engulf.

Sylvia drew herself up to her full height and fixed Winthrop with a gaze sharp enough to pierce his smarm and silence his lip. "No one knows a Wunk's true appearance," she declaimed, "for they can change form at will. It is said that they can even take on the shape of a person, and can thus walk among us, for they enjoy human company, though they are themselves terribly shy." She paused long enough to shove her fascinator back out of her face before continuing, "as to the footprints, that is how I know it was a Wunk. You see, they are so shy that they cannot stand to be seen. Even if they are not in their natural form, they hate to be noticed unless they themselves have already chosen to be out and about and thus have braced themselves for the experience. If someone spots a Wunk when they are not ready for interaction, and they realize they have been seen, they immediately panic and hide."

"So they run away?" someone asked. "Wouldn't that just make more footprints?"

"Aha!" The bedraggled grand dame waggled a finger at the speaker. "You would think so, would you not? But that is not how a Wunk works! No, they do not run, they hide—and they do that by digging a hole in the ground, diving into it, and pulling the hole in after them!" She finished that last with a flourish and studied the crowd, clearly expecting praise for this startling revelation. Instead, she was met with stunned silence, followed after a moment by a single loud guffaw.

It was Winthrop, of course. "They pull the hole in after them?" he repeated, his volume increasing with each word. "So there's no sign they were ever there? Oh, that's capital, it is! Look, Pat" —he turned to Mercer, who was attempting to disappear by not moving a muscle— "Sylvia here has solved the case for you! It's a Wunk that was your witness, and it hid once Trevor spotted it! It all makes perfect sense!"

That had the room roaring at last, at Sylvia and Mercer both. The latter dwindled, shrinking in on himself and attempting to slink away, though the laughter followed him out. The former merely *harrumph*ed and fixed her steely eyes upon Winthrop until he found his own humor sticking in his throat.

"That," Sylvia stated once the amusement had faded enough for her to be heard again, as her voice had fallen back out of declamatory mode and resumed its usual tremulous warble, "is the problem with youth today. You refuse to believe that which you cannot see and spend yourself, and do not accept the wisdom of your elders. Mark my words, one day you will wish you had listened and heeded more and mocked far less!" With that ominous warning, she finally sank back down into her chair, taking a large gulp from the fresh cocktail the butler had just helpfully provided.

No one quite knew what to make of Sylvia's pronouncement, though Bridget preened slightly, congratulating herself on cultivating a relationship with just such a wise elder and thus placing herself in a position to be the only one benefiting from that accumulated knowledge. Even she did not see a way to reconcile that with this latest information, however, and so the talk quickly turned from Sylvia's mysterious Wunk to the sad state of her fascinator, and from there to talk of the latest fascinator styles emerging from Paris.

Few of the attendees noticed another figure who had stood in the doorway during Sylvia's recitation. If they had, they might have been surprised, as so many of them had recently remarked on this particular person's unexpected appearance and odd behavior, coupled with her similarity to the recently deceased Miss Barnes. Instead, no one really noticed as the young lady named Winnie surveyed the room, her mild gray gaze seeming to take in every detail. Nor did they notice the gentle, almost mocking smile that played across her pale lips before she slipped away again.

The only person who did notice her, in fact, was Sylvia, whose vision was no longer obscured by her unfortunate headpiece. That older lady's eyes followed the quiet young woman's departure from the room, and if a knowing smile touched her gaze and lips, it was well-hidden by the glass she quickly drained. Her only comment on the moment was to hold that same glass high and demand a refill, which was swiftly provided.

CHAPTER SEVEN

While this strange knowledge was being imparted within the house, Detective Davis had not been idle outside of its confines. After Mercer had returned to regale the other guests with his amazing discovery, the police inspector had stayed outside, considering. There were no other traces of this mysterious witness to be found, it was true, but that did not mean the lawn and the woods could not yield any useful information.

"What exactly can we tell from where she died?" he asked aloud, causing Carruthers and Grant to exchange a glance. The two officers remained silent, however, unsure if their superior had been speaking to them or to himself. The latter seemed to be the case, as he crouched and studied the scene of Lisette Barnes's demise once more.

"We can see that she fell here," Davis muttered, resting his hand just above the depression caused by the young woman's body hitting the ground and compacting dirt and grass beneath her. "Which means whoever killed her had to be standing... here." He stood and paced a slow circle around that indentation, describing the distance a reasonably sized individual would have had to stand within to wrap hands around the young woman's slender throat. "So, if that's the case, where did they come from?" He considered the surrounding area again. The most direct path to the house was to walk straight from the French doors, as he and the others had already done. That route was well-trod, so much so that any specific prints had been obliterated between the rush of others. *Had that been deliberate?* he wondered. Could the killer have been among those men and encouraged the others to retrace his steps with him to conceal his tracks? Trevor Kinkaid had been one of them.

But what if the killer had not been among them? That would mean he had not known the men would walk that way, which meant he couldn't have counted on them to conceal evidence of his passage. Perhaps, then, he would have taken a different approach to this spot, one that was not as obvious and thus less likely to be spotted? Davis dismissed the side that backed up against the woods—even if someone had reached Lisette from there, they would be almost impossible to trace through the leaves and twigs, as the mysterious witness's foot-steps proved. That left paths to either side. On the left, walking would mean skirting along the outer edge of Trevor's property, well away from the house—easier to conceal yourself, perhaps, but a good deal farther to go. On the right, it meant coming from the house but farther along than the sitting room. That was more likely to be seen since you would be walking behind the house the whole way, but it was also easier to exit somewhere else along the building and approach from that side—and, if you were careful, you would never cross in front of the French doors, which were the likeliest place from which you might be seen.

Given that logic, Davis concentrated along the right side—and nodded once, pleased with his own reasoning, when his search turned up a clear row of footprints, pressed deep into the soft ground and completely untrampled as they were from a direction rarely taken.

"Come have a look at this," he called, and Carruthers quickly joined him to examine the marks.

"Man's boots," the officer stated at once, no doubt evident in his tone. "Though—odd." Which they were. The front and back edges of the footprints were blurred and indistinct, as if the person making them had slipped with each and every step. The ground was damp, it was true, and no doubt had been even softer a few hours ago before the sun had dried it more, but that also seemed odd to Davis. Still, there was no question Carruthers was right. The prints had been made by a man's boot. More specifically, the treads were from a pair of galoshes, just the thing for traipsing through mud and water. Davis set his own foot beside the nearest pair. Because of the blurring, it was difficult to tell, but he'd estimate they were a size nine at least, and perhaps a ten. Not abnormal but not small, either.

"Thanks, Carruthers. Stay with Grant," Davis instructed, and began following the footprints back away from the scene. They were easy enough to see, even in the fading light, and soon enough he had shadowed them around the corner of the house—and to a side door. It opened onto a portico, and within the tidy little whitewashed porch Davis saw a bench with hooks above it for coats and hats and a shelf below for boots, holders on either side for umbrellas and canes. Only a few items were present, for this entrance would not be available to guests, only household members and staff.

One of the pairs of footwear under the bench, however, was a set of men's galoshes. Size ten, he confirmed when he lifted them out, and with soles that matched the marks outside.

They even still had fresh mud stuck between the treads.

One of the kitchen staff had opened the intervening door upon hearing Davis enter. "Ask your master to meet me here," Davis instructed. "Immediately." The woman bowed and backed away, and it was only a few moments later that the door swung open again, this time revealing Trevor Kinkaid behind it.

"You sent for me, Detective?" His tone was truculent, that of a man not used to being summoned by anyone, and especially not in his own house, yet he had responded quickly enough, and there was no hesitation in his tone or guilt evident in his face as he joined the inspector out on the rough plank floor of the portico by the bench.

"Whose are these?" Davis asked, holding the boots up for inspection.

"Mine," Trevor answered after only a glance. "I wear them when I'm trekking in the rain, and when exercising the dogs." He frowned. "Why?"

The detective answered that question with another one: "And when was the last time you wore them?"

His host's frown deepened, though it seemed more from thought than irritation. "Monday, I think," he answered after a moment. "Yes, Monday—we had that big storm and one of the trees out back lost a limb. I went out with Carl, my groundskeeper, to check the damage. Why?"

Davis did not bother to answer. Instead he stood, still holding the galoshes, and carried them with him as he passed through the kitchen and down the service corridor into the main body of the house. He returned to the study and set the boots down on the floor beside the desk, carefully laying them on their side so as not to disturb the evidence collected in their soles.

"Thank you," he finally told Trevor. "I'll let you know if I need anything else." The older man *harrumph*ed but, when it was clear he would not be told anything more, excused himself to see to his guests and to dinner, which would be served shortly.

Once he was alone, Davis sighed. The boots were strong evidence, but hardly enough — they had been easily accessible, and anyone could have pulled them on. He would need more to go on if he were to make any charges stick. And since he had no other physical evidence to work with at the moment, he would have to switch gears and focus on testimony and character reports instead.

With that in mind, he ventured forth from the study, seeking out some of the people he had already seen at the party. The first one he came across was, of course, none other than Pat Mercer, who might be said to have been lurking nearby for exactly such a purpose.

"Mr. Mercer, wasn't it?" Davis asked as he approached the younger man, who affected surprise at being recognized so accurately.

"Yes, that's correct," he answered, nothing loathe. "Patrick Thomas Mercer, Esquire, at your service." He offered his hand, which proved to be limp and fine-boned, the skin perfectly smooth. "What can I do for you, Detective?"

"I was hoping you might answer a few questions," Davis replied. He gestured toward the study. "Would you mind?"

"Not at all." Mercer followed him in and took one of the armchairs as Davis settled himself behind the desk as if he had grown up there. "What is it you'd like to know?" The man preened a bit at being asked for his expert opinion.

Across from him, the detective steepled his fingers. "What can you tell me about Lisette Barnes and Trevor Kinkaid?"

"As a couple, you mean?" Mercer threw back his head and laughed. "Oh, Trevor wishes! But Lisette — Miss Barnes — wasn't having any of it! He followed her around all day long, like a puppy dog, all big eyes and drool, and she'd occasionally reward him with a pat on the head, but he wasn't getting any belly rubs, if you take my meaning." Mercer chuckled again, pleased with his own metaphor and resolving to file that one away for further use later. "No, as far as she was concerned, Trevor was just a rich man she could sponge food and drink off. A means to an end, if you will."

"So they weren't together?" Davis restated. "You're sure of that? Not before this party, either?"

"Oh, quite sure." Mercer sat back, cocking one leg over the other and hooking both hands around his knee, the picture of relaxed confidence. "This was the first time she'd been a guest here, you see. She was a fresh commodity, which is, of course, part of why Trevor was so interested. He's had a go at most of the other women here, and only been turned away by a handful, if that many. But they all knew him and his habits. Lisette didn't, which made her fair game."

"I see." Davis considered that. "Did you see how things ended between them today?"

"Not directly, no," the younger man admitted sadly, clearly disappointed he had missed out on such high drama. "But when I first saw Trevor without Lisette flitting ahead of him, he looked like someone had just shot his favorite dog. Completely despondent." He shook his head. "Then, of course, she turned up dead. Terrible, absolutely terrible." He leaned forward. "So, did he kill her, do you reckon?"

Davis offered a bland, noncommittal smile in return. "I'm afraid I can't make any suppositions," he replied. "But thank you for your time, sir. It's greatly appreciated." He rose, forcing Mercer to do so as well, and led the way to the door, opening it and showing the man out. "If I have any further questions, I'll be sure to let you know."

Mercer stomped off in a huff, annoyed to not have been praised more for his participation or included farther into the details of the investigation, but Davis was unconcerned about that. His attention had already settled on another man he recognized, the earnest Will Lowder. Will was genuinely surprised to be asked into the study, but complied quickly enough, and seemed happy to help, if only he knew how.

"Oh, I didn't really know her at all," he answered when asked about the late Miss Barnes. "None of us did — it was her first time here." He smiled. "She seemed nice, though. Sweet, you know? A lot of the ladies here, they're more..." He paused, struggling to find the right word. Several came immediately to Davis's mind, but he did not offer any of them, waiting to see what his interviewee came up with instead. "Complicated," was the final result, though Will's frown indicated he was not entirely happy with that himself. "Or, you know, just they're used to things, they've seen it all, they're kinda bored with everything. Takes a lot to impress them." He scratched behind his ear. "But Lisette, she was all smiles. Everything was new and exciting to her. I thought that was nice."

"And her and Trevor?" Davis asked.

Will sighed and looked down at his hands—which, Davis had noticed, bore the calluses and chapping of someone who actually used them, even if just for tennis and swimming. "Oh, he thought she was nice, too," he admitted softly, his tone that of a boy who does not want to tattle but feels compelled to answer truthfully. "And she liked him just fine, but maybe not... fully, you know? She was nice about it, though. She wasn't mean at all. And they smiled and laughed a lot, the whole day. I saw them."

"But nothing more than that?" Davis pressed. "No kissing, holding hands, anything else?"

"Oh, no," Will said immediately. "She didn't seem the sort. I mean"—and he actually blushed, which was an impressive feat, considering the company he kept— "she seemed like a good girl, you know? Not the kind who'd just... let someone take liberties."

Davis nodded. "Thank you," he said, as gently as he could, for it was clear the other man was already nearly overwhelmed with grief for this girl he had hardly known. "I really appreciate your help."

Interestingly, Will then turned teary eyes toward him and asked the same question Mercer had, though with very different intent. "Do you think he did that to her?" he managed to choke out, and Davis had to resist the urge to comfort the younger man. Such duties did occasionally come with the job, but this was not the time or place. He did not, however, brush the question off as he had the last time.

"I don't know yet," he answered instead, getting to his feet and heading toward the study door. "But I promise you, I intend to find out."

Will nodded and allowed himself to be shepherded out of the room. "Good," he said as he slipped back into the hall. "She deserves that."

Davis could not have agreed more.

CHAPTER EIGHT

The detective cast about, once Will had left, trying to decide whom to interview next. In doing so, his attention was drawn to a minor commotion taking place in one of the other rooms.

Stepping out of the study and shutting it behind him, he followed the noise to a nearby drawing room, where a handful of people were speaking, several of them with raised voices. One of those, he was hardly surprised to discover, was Pat Mercer.

"I am telling you," Mercer was insisting heatedly, "that Trevor is the one who killed her! I had that directly from the inspector himself!"

Annoyed at this usurpation of his name, Davis began forward, opening his mouth to speak and to dress the arrogant young man down once and for all. Before he could, however, a softer voice arose, cutting through the tumult easily despite its gentler register and milder volume.

"I find that difficult to believe," the speaker declared. "It seems highly unlikely, in fact." She was of average height and built, Davis ascertained, and mildly attractive features, with light brown hair and warm grey eyes—and more than a passing similarity to the dead woman, for indeed this was none other than the infamous Winnie. "Perhaps," she continued now, "we should simply ask the detective himself." And with that, she turned her gaze full upon Davis, making him the center of attention—for everyone save Mercer, who quickly peered about, seeking some avenue of escape.

That was not to be, however. "Indeed," Davis replied, letting his voice rise to fill the space, "you are correct, madam. I did not say such a thing, nor would I. What I did tell Mr. Mercer is that this is an ongoing police investigation, and as such, I cannot possibly comment on anyone's guilt or innocence." His own glare slammed into the younger man as if it were a sledgehammer, forcing him back a step and nearly driving him to his knees. "But perhaps Mr. Mercer misunderstood me."

"Ah." Mercer was not fool enough to miss the lifeline that had just been thrown his way, nor was he slow to grasp for it. "Yes, that must be it. Terribly sorry, Detective. I would never deliberately put words in your mouth or attempt to influence an official investigation."

"See that you do not," he was warned, "for obstruction of justice is a serious crime, in and of itself, and a charge I will not hesitate to lay upon anyone who does willfully seek to influence my progress or my findings." Davis let that threat hang in the air a moment before offering a smile to drain away some of its dreadful impact. "Now, if you'll all excuse me, I still have work to do." He began to turn away, then paused. "Miss, perhaps you'd be so kind as to accompany me?" That last was directed toward Winnie, who nodded and quickly extricated herself from the crowd, following him back to the study, where they were both quickly ensconced.

"What can I do for you, Detective?" she asked, seating herself in one of the armchairs. Something about her manner was so forthright, so disarming, that Davis surprised himself by taking the matching chair rather than his now-customary place behind the desk. Up close, he had more of an opportunity to study this young lady. She was attractive, certainly, though not as vividly as Lisette Barnes had been, even in death. Winnie's charm was quieter, calmer, less entrancing, but more calming. Her dress was, as has been said, a dove gray, but in style and cut it was actually superior to that of the deceased, being more a match to Bridget's and thus more in the latest fashion. Her fascinator, while simpler and not as tall, was also quite stylish, and both that and her other jewelry were of high quality, as if either she had had the first choice of accessories or had simply made the wiser purchases. She did carry a faint hint of perfume, which her sister apparently had not, but it was not a scent Davis recognized, smelling almost of pine and clove rather than the more usual floral notes. It suited her, however, seeming clean and fresh and natural.

"I understand," Davis began, "that you have been asking questions." He smiled to show that he was not angry before adding, "I do believe that to be my job."

"Of course." She smiled in return, and it was shy and sweet and fleeting. "I apologize if I am interfering. I sought only to help."

"I believe your name is Winnie, is it not?" was his next question, to which she dipped her head.

"You may call me that, yes."

"And you are Miss Lisette Barnes's sister?"

Winnie looked away, worrying her lower lip with small, neat teeth. "She is — was — my responsibility."

An odd way to phrase it, Davis thought, but it matched with his impression that Winnie was the elder of the two. "I am very sorry for your loss." She dipped her head in thanks. "Normally, Miss Barnes, I would ask that you cease your questioning and let me do my job unopposed." He sighed. "But in a case like this, with so many people to question and only myself to cover them all, I believe it's better to make use of you, at least insofar as anything you've already learned." He waited a second before prompting, "Have you learned anything?"

"Oh!" She started a little. "I'm sorry. I didn't realize that was an actual question. Well, yes. Perhaps. Maybe." She twisted her hands together. "That is, I'm not sure."

For a second, there was silence as she composed her thoughts. Then she met his gaze with her own. "Lisette spent much of the day with Mister Kinkaid, but I'm sure you've already learned that. She had his full attention, or as much of it as any good host could spare. And it was not unappreciated but not entirely returned, either — everyone says the same. He was far more enamored of her than she was of him."

"Is that common for your sister?" Davis asked. "Was she cool toward her admirers, or was there something about Trevor in particular that caused her to not reciprocate fully? His age, or some other factor?"

"I don't know," Winnie answered, shaking her head. "I'm afraid I cannot offer any real insights into Lisette's personality or behavior. We... were not close."

Ah, Davis thought, his policeman's mind slotting that detail into place. *Some sort of falling out between the sisters, and now she feels misplaced guilt over her sister's death. Of course.* Outwardly, he said nothing, merely waited for her to continue.

"I'm sure you know that this was Lisette's first visit to this house, and first attendance at one of these parties," Winnie stated when she felt comfortable taking up the narrative again. "No one here knew her beforehand, except perhaps whoever it was who first invited her — I know someone did, but I don't know who. Not Trevor, though. He'd never seen her before today."

Davis nodded. "I'd heard much the same," he confirmed. "I will need to track down whoever did invite her and learn the details, though. Let me know if you find out who it was." He shook his head. "But with that being the case, it seems unlikely anyone else could have reason to harm your sister, much less kill her." *Unless perhaps you did*, his mind offered, unable to ignore the possibility, particularly since most murders were committed by family. Still, he could not easily accept the idea that this demure young lady before him could be capable of such a violent crime.

"You are thinking that it looks bad for Mister Kinkaid," Winnie offered, misinterpreting his frown but only slightly, as that would have been his next apprehension. "But I ask you, why would he kill her? What would he possibly have to gain from such an action?"

"She spurned his advances," Davis pointed out, but his companion scoffed, waving the claim away.

"He is a grown man, powerful and wealthy," she argued. "He had no shortage of companions available — why not soothe his wounded pride by turning to one of them? Why follow Lisette out of doors and throttle her? That's an extreme reaction! It might be different if they had been lovers for many a month and then she had suddenly thrown him over for another, but they'd only just met!"

"Perhaps, but he is a proud man. And wounded pride can lead to extreme responses, even violent ones. Maybe he saw her out there and, still angry, went after her to vent some of his rage — she shouted back, he grew even more incensed, and finally snapped."

"Maybe, but from what I've seen and heard so far, that's out of character," Winnie stated. "Everyone I've spoken to agrees that Mister Kinkaid can be a trifle terse, a touch arrogant, a tad overbearing, but they've never seen him lose his temper, never seen him shout, and certainly never seen him lift a hand toward anyone."

Davis frowned, tapping his chin. "If only I could find that witness Trevor claims he saw! That would help a great deal! I don't suppose you've got anything on who that might be?"

But Winnie shook her head. "I wouldn't put too much hope in finding them," she warned. "I'd think that, if anyone had seen something, they'd have come forward by now."

Which was exactly what Davis had thought himself, though he did not say so. Still, he knew from long experience that people's conscience could weigh upon them more and more as time went on. That meant there was still a chance for any witness to find their courage and do the right thing, though the window of opportunity was dwindling rapidly.

"Well, it seems we've found much the same things so far," he told the young lady beside him after a moment. "I appreciate the confirmation, if nothing else."

"I'm sorry I couldn't be more help," she replied, rising to her feet. She was the first of his interviewees besides Trevor himself to make the move to end the meeting instead of waiting to be dismissed, but then their conversation had been more casual, more collegial, and thus she may not have felt the same pressure to wait for his permission to depart.

As it was, Davis saw no reason to detain her any longer. "I would ask that you refrain as much as possible from questioning people further," he said, standing as well and making for the door a few paces behind her. He smiled. "Or at least that you keep me informed of anything you discover."

She returned the smile. "I absolutely will," she promised, sliding the door open just enough to slip through and leaving him to wonder which of the two options she had just indicated she would follow.

He had little time to debate that, however, as a new figure appeared at the door almost at once. "Detective Davis? I'd hoped we might have a word."

The newcomer was tall for a woman, and not as willowy as some, with strong features that could better be defined as "striking" and "commanding" rather than pretty. Her attire was first-rate, however, a striking platinum dress cut of the finest cloth and in the latest fashion, and she wore it with the casual arrogance of one born to money and power. Her dark hair, though cut stylishly short and curled, still bore a similar color to her father's, and her jaw was a smaller version of his own, as were her nose and brow. Thus, Davis knew her even before she introduced herself as "Daphne Kinkaid."

"Ah, of course—please come in, Miss Kinkaid." Davis shut the doors again behind her as she strolled in as if she owned the place, the rich scent of vanilla and bergamot floating along behind her. Indeed, by the time he'd turned around she had already placed herself behind her father's desk, sprawling in the chair there with one leg hiked insouciantly over the arm. Deciding that it would be gauche for him to demand she surrender that seat, the detective contented himself with returning to the chair he had just occupied beside Winnie, though now he leaned back to match this new woman's attitude of nonchalance. "What can I do for you?" he asked.

"I think it is more what I can do for you," she answered with a taut smile. "You have been asking questions about my father, of course. And who better to answer them than me?"

"Anything you can tell me would be helpful," Davis agreed. "Both about his temperament in general and about his relationship with Miss Barnes."

"Relationship? Ha!" Daphne's laugh was similar to her father's as well, strong and full. "What relationship? They met earlier today, he was immediately smitten, she strung him along for a bit and then got bored with the way he was drooling over her, she cut him loose and he reacted badly to it. I think that more than adequately sums it up."

"When you say 'reacted badly,'" the detective repeated carefully, "you are suggesting..."

"That he followed her when she fled the house, screamed at her, and, when she tried to escape into the woods, grabbed her and strangled her?" Daphne paused, one gloved hand flying to her mouth as if attempting belatedly to call back the words that had just spilled forth. "Well, it does seem that way, doesn't it?" she finally confirmed with a shudder. "Please understand, I love my father dearly, but he does have a temper, and he can lose control at times." She did not meet the inspector's eyes. "I'm afraid it would not be the first time."

"I see." Davis digested this new information, stroking his chin. "I have to tell you, Miss Kinkaid, I'm surprised to hear that. It does not match what I've heard from your father's guests thus far."

She shrugged that off. "They don't really know him, though, do they? They're just rabble he surrounds himself with from time to time so that he can bask in their admiration. He's careful to be on his best behavior at his parties because he knows how quickly rumors can spread. No one can get wind of the fact that Trevor Kinkaid occasionally likes to hit women." She rubbed her arms, shrinking in on herself slightly.

"Yes, of course." He kept his tone as gentle as possible. "Well, thank you for coming forward, ma'am. That does cast things in a different light."

The lady behind the desk sighed. "I hate to have to," she answered. "But he's gone too far this time. It's just awful what happened to that poor young woman!"

"It is indeed." Davis rose to his feet, coming around the desk and offering his hand. She had little choice but to take it and allow him to help her stand and then lead her toward the door. Impressively, her eye makeup remained unsmudged despite the emotional confession she had just made. "Thank you again," he told her as he saw her out. "I appreciate your honesty and your courage."

"Of course." She nodded, sniffling only a little. "Please let me know if there's anything else I can do to help." Then she was gone, leaving the detective alone with his thoughts, his theories—and a momentous decision to make.

CHAPTER NINE

Next, the detective went in search of his host. By virtue of asking a butler, he eventually found the man in one of the smaller rooms off the main hall. It was a comparatively tiny space well-lined with bookcases and furnished only with four armchairs, accompanying side tables, and a standing globe that Davis suspected contained liquor. It was a nook well-suited to private conversations and even assignations, though at the moment, it seemed its occupants were more inclined toward the former than the latter. Trevor was there, along with a similarly aged gentleman Davis had seen earlier and a woman of equal vintage. The lady was sipping at a drink that was clearly not water or lemonade and the second gentleman had an equally potable-looking amber liquid in a large crystal tumbler. Trevor himself had only his customary coffee mug, though what that contained was anyone's guess.

"Pardon me," Davis stated as he entered, causing all three to break off whatever they had been discussing to focus their full attention upon him. "I'm sorry to interrupt."

"No need," the woman replied breezily, waving her cigarette holder and leaving a trail of smoke from the cigarette affixed at its tip. The small room was already thick with the scent of smoke mixed with her Chanel and cut by the sharp tang of whiskey. "We were merely reminiscing. The danger of being around old folk, don't you know? So much of our lives are already behind us that we cannot resist showing off the breadth and depth of them and recalling those halcyon days when we were ourselves still young and vibrant."

Trevor had risen to his feet. "Detective Allan Davis, allow me to introduce Doctor Daniel Halsey and Madam Sylvia Beaumont. Two of my oldest and dearest friends." That last was said with obvious warmth, and both of his companions smiled fondly in return.

"Oh?" Davis had been intent upon a different path but now saw an opportunity not to be missed. "I would very much like to speak to each of you, then. If you wouldn't mind?"

"Of course," the doctor answered. "Happy to help. Did you wish to speak here?"

"I can step out into the hall," their host offered gallantly and without a hint of trepidation. "That way, you can speak to both of them freely."

"That might be easiest, thank you," the detective agreed. He waited until Trevor had exited the room and shut the heavy oak door behind him, then took one of the two vacant armchairs. They were exceedingly comfortable, as indeed all of the house was, showing that the owner was a man who firmly believed that utility was just as important as appearance, and that quality did not require showiness.

"You want to know about the dead girl," Halsey stated baldly once Davis had settled in. "I was one of those who found her, you know."

"Oh?" Davis glanced at Sylvia, who shook her head.

"I was still in the sitting room," she answered his unspoken question. "Doing exactly what that room is best for — sitting. None of the women felt like risking our expensive shoes by traipsing through the wet grass, so we waited until the men had returned and then got the full story from them." She shook her head. "Awful business, though. And such a pretty young thing — not that being pretty should make any sort of a difference, but of course, if we're being quite honest, it does, doesn't it? We always lament the loss of someone attractive more than someone unappealing. Shallow, but that's human nature."

Davis found he could hardly disagree with that, though he had rarely heard it stated so openly. There was something almost admirable about the lady's willingness to expose such human foibles. "I would like to hear what you saw," he told the doctor now, "but honestly the thing I am most interested in from the two of you is a description of Mister Kinkaid's character, and anything you can tell me about him and Miss Barnes."

The older folk glanced at each other, and there was in that look an instant of naked complicity, two friends uniting to protect a third from the suspicions of an outsider. But, just as plainly, they both then set that aside. "I've known Trevor Kinkaid for over twenty-five years," Halsey started plainly. "We met at school, you see. He was there to study law, and he did get his degree in it, though only barely, and I don't think he's ever really used it. I was there for medicine, of course. We did rugby together, and crew, and became friends. Stayed in touch after school, and after a few years, both wound up in this area, which is when we truly reconnected. I don't think we've gone more than two weeks without seeing each other since, unless one of us was away somewhere."

"I met him a bit more recently than all that, though still quite some time ago," Sylvia took up the story. "My late husband Mitchell was at school with the two of them, and I met both Trevor and Daniel at our wedding." She smiled, a misty look of recalling distant memories. "The three of them were nearly inseparable, and so it was fortunate that I found I liked them as well, and that they decided to tolerate me, else I'd rarely have seen my own spouse!"

That coaxed a laugh from Halsey, and Davis could see that this was an old routine, well-worn and still amusing. "So that was not hyperbole on his part," he commented, gesturing toward the door and the absent Trevor. "You have both known him longer than anyone else here." They nodded. "How would you describe him, then?"

"Stubborn," Halsey answered at once. "Stubborn as a mule. Once he sets his mind to a thing, good luck trying to change it! He won't shift for all the tea in China!"

"Yes, and independent, too," Sylvia added. "He hates to ask for help, absolutely hates it. When his wife Helen died, some twelve years ago now, I had to practically beat him before he would admit he had no idea how to handle their daughter. Daphne was just a girl then, not even in her teens, and here was Trevor trying to raise her alone without having the first idea how! He did better with his son, Michael, but then he'd been a boy himself once, hadn't he? That was something he could understand! But a girl? He hadn't a clue, but he refused to admit it!"

"Oh, yes, Trevor's always been proud," the doctor agreed, striking a match and sticking the flame into the bowl of his pipe, which had gone out. "But he's loyal, too. Always there for his friends, no matter what."

"That he is." Sylvia sighed and took a deep gulp of her drink—Davis deliberately ignored the smell of alcohol wafting from both the cup and its owner. "When Mitchell died, I don't mind telling you, I fell all apart. It was Trevor and Daniel who saw me through it. Most of my female friends deserted me—oh, they made sympathetic noises, sent fruit baskets, invited me to tea, but they didn't actually want to be bothered with any of the messy details. These two," she gazed fondly at her friend, patting him on the shoulder and producing a flushed but pleased smile in response, "they weren't worried about getting their hands dirty or about being seen as unmanly for consoling a bereft woman. I don't know what I would have done without them."

Davis nodded, his attention fully on Sylvia. "You said when his wife died Trevor was left to raise Daphne alone, but for your help. How did that go? Do they get on well?"

"Ah." For the first time, she seemed reticent to answer. "Well, you know, the relationship between a father and daughter, it can be tricky."

Halsey was less circumspect. "Especially when the girl's an un-grateful little snot," he declared with a snort. "Sorry, but that's the plain truth. Trevor doted on her and Michael both, tried his best, gave them everything, but Daphne, she's as willful as he is and didn't like him reining her in. They'd argue all the time, mainly over her excesses and outbursts. Finally, he had no choice but to cut her off."

"Cut her off?" That did come as a surprise to the policeman. "She didn't say anything about that."

His comment clearly startled his two companions in return. "Daphne's here?" Sylvia blurted out. "Oh, of course, she is — that child has always had spectacularly awful timing. I wonder if Trevor knows — I don't think they've spoken in at least a year, possibly two."

"More like two, indeed," Halsey agreed. "And no, I doubt he does, or he'd have told us." Pulling his pipe from his lips, he used it like a pointer to indicate both himself and the lady with him. "We're the last ones Daphne'd want to see," he explained. "We're her godparents, and she knows we're none too pleased with her behavior of late."

"I see." And Davis thought perhaps he did, though that did not necessarily negate the other things he'd been told. "I hate to ask this," he began, "because clearly it is delicate, and you are his friends, but in your opinion, do you think it at all possible that Trevor could have —"

He did not finish, for Halsey cut him off. "Not a chance," the doctor stated firmly. "In all the years I've known him, Trevor has never been violent. Not toward anyone."

"What?" It took Sylvia a second or two longer to catch on to the drift of their conversation, most likely due to the drink she had emptied, and however many had gone before that one, but when she did, she straightened in pure and undisguised outrage. "Absolutely not!" she agreed fervently. "Trevor Kinkaid is one of the kindest, gentlest men I have ever met! Even when he is angry — and it is rare — the worst I have ever seen or heard him do was raise his voice, throw a glass into the fireplace, and one time overturn a chair! In all the years, no matter how he fought with Daphne, he never once laid a hand on the girl — though if you ask me, a few spankings might have helped a great deal! And he's never been rough with a woman. I don't think he's ever even gotten into a fistfight!"

"There was one, back in college," Halsey corrected, calming down a bit now that they were referring to the ancient past once more. "A fellow from a rival school made some unflattering remarks about our rowing team — and then had the bad manners to comment on the team captain's girlfriend. The captain was not there, and Trevor felt honor-bound to reply." He grinned a bit ruefully. "His nose eventually recovered, but he swore he'd never get into a situation like that again."

Davis leaned back. "So you're saying that Miss Barnes... the way she died..."

"Not a chance," the doctor repeated. "Trevor could never have done that. Not to anyone, much less a woman he'd only just met."

"I agree completely," Sylvia declared. "You need to find that witness and ask them, they'll confirm it. Find the Wunk."

Halsey rolled his eyes at that, but Davis still had to ask: "I'm sorry, the what?"

"No, the Wunk," she said again. "Your missing witness. It's a Wunk."

She explained about the mysterious, secretive creature, while the doctor mimed drinking behind her back. Davis was not entirely sure what to make of that. The old lady had seemed utterly lucid until that moment, and he had certainly heard of stranger creatures in terms of local folklore. No one had ever claimed them to be real, however, nor suggested they could be involved in, much less integral, to a murder investigation!

"I will certainly take that under advisement," he told Sylvia after she had finished. "And I promise you, we are making every effort to track down that witness, no matter who it may be." He pushed back the chair and stood. "Thank you both for your time and your insight. It's greatly appreciated." And he exited the room, slightly less convinced of the accuracy of their character report on their friend after the old lady's assertion that a supernatural creature might somehow be involved. Still, the doctor had seemed wholly rational, as she had otherwise, so he couldn't discount their opinion completely. He almost wished he could, as it would make all this a good deal easier.

Chapter Ten

Some policemen were of the type who enjoyed toying with people. They took to the job because it gave them authority over others and the ability to intimidate, bully, manipulate, and frighten people, particularly those being treated as suspects but also sometimes those who were witnesses and occasionally even victims. Men of this type did sometimes prove to be effective officers because, at times, they used this ability to get to the truth, even when those they questioned were unwilling to provide it. More often, however, this brand of policeman was more interested in producing fear than in actually pursuing justice, and though they often closed their cases, it was entirely possible that their culprits were simply those who had been most easily manipulated into confessing to the crime, or those upon whom it had been easiest to pin the evidence.

Fortunately, Allan Davis was not of this sort. He believed in justice, and truth, and fair play. As such, he felt after speaking to Halsey and Sylvia that it was his duty to seek out the very man they had discussed and to lay out the situation as he saw it, and the action he now felt compelled to take.

Dinner was being served, and so Davis found Trevor easily enough, as the older man was overseeing the meal. The dining room possessed a grand table capable of seating twenty, but even this was nowhere near sufficient to hold the number of guests present for one of his parties, so instead, that impressive surface was merely used as the buffet table, with dishes arranged in a neat row along its top. The chairs had all been pulled away to allow easier access to the food, placed against the walls instead, and dishes and plates were set on smaller tables to either side. Drinks were arrayed upon the sideboard, coffee and tea and water and lemonade along with other, more potent beverages, and it was perhaps a mark of this group's assumption of invulnerability that they had not even attempted to hide away such liquids upon the police's arrival, though of course that had hardly been anyone's chief priority at the time. Regardless, things were set up so that guests could wander in, fill their plates—a novel experience in and of itself, serving themselves, though of course there were household staff stationed along the table to do the actual dishing out, it was merely that the guests had to suffer the unusual and slightly titillating experience of holding the plates themselves—refresh their drinks, and then drift through the house, seeking an adequate place to sit and eat amongst agreeable company. The home was large enough that something like ten rooms were available on the first floor alone, and so everyone could easily find a place to dine either alone or with a group, however they preferred.

Davis's appearance in the dining room caused a bit of a stir, of course. Not all the guests had seen him upon his arrival, but all had heard of him by now, and it was clear that this sober-looking man, in his equally sober (and clearly rack-bought) suit, was not one of their own and therefore must be the detective in question. They parted before him, allowing him easy and unobstructed access to the room, and he strode in, heading straight for Trevor. The stares and whispers he ignored, as indeed he was used to such behavior in his line of work.

"Ah, Detective," the older man exclaimed upon seeing him. "Can I interest you in some dinner?" He gestured at the lavish spread. "Please, help yourself. And can I send some food out to your men? They shouldn't starve just because they are doing their job."

It was on the tip of his tongue to refuse, but three things stopped Davis from doing so. The first was that his host was absolutely correct, Carruthers and the others should not be penalized for their diligence. He himself had often bought lunch or dinner for the men while they were working a case, both to make sure they did have an opportunity to eat and to keep them from getting distracted or leaving the scene. There was no real reason to refuse Trevor's generous offer, and it would certainly make everything simpler.

The second reason was that Davis had dealt with people, particularly powerful men, enough to know that refusing would create animosity, which would only make his job more difficult. Far better to accept, and thus keep Trevor happy and willing to assist the investigation as much as possible.

The third reason was simply that, although he made a decent wage and lived frugally enough, Davis could hardly be said to lead a life of extravagance, and the smells arising from the buffet had his mouth watering and his stomach growling.

So "Thank you, that's very kind and much appreciated" was what he said instead, as he accepted the plate Trevor offered him and turned to the nearest butler, who stood behind a long silver serving dish heaped with steaming-hot slices of roast beef.

After filling his plate and taking a tall glass of iced tea to accompany it, Davis at last focused on his host instead of his dinner. "Again, thank you," he began. "But I wonder if we might have a quick word as well?"

"Of course." Without needing to confer, Trevor led the way back to his own study, exactly as Davis had been about to suggest. There they resumed their previous places, Davis setting the plate and glass down on the desktop just to one side. He had already noticed that the glass top would protect the actual furniture from any moisture rings or stains and was careful not to place the items too near any papers, either.

"First of all, I want to thank you for being so accommodating, and so cooperative," Davis said. "Not everyone is in such circumstances, and it does make my job a good deal easier."

"Hm." Trevor waved the compliment off. "I can't imagine how one could do otherwise. Horrible situation, and of course, I want to see justice done."

"You'd be surprised," was all the detective replied. He folded his hands together before him, almost as if he were praying, and sighed. "I have to tell you, though, that it does not look good for you right now." He held up one hand to forestall the other man's protestations of innocence. "You are the last person we can prove saw Miss Barnes alive," he pointed out. "You spent much of the day wooing her, and by your own admission, those efforts were then spurned. In addition to which, I've found your galoshes, which bear fresh mud showing they were used today, and match the prints leading to and from the crime scene." Trevor started at that, though whether from surprise or guilt, Davis could not tell. "I've had conflicting reports on your temperament—"

That was enough to make Trevor forget his manners. "Conflicting?" he interrupted. "What do you mean? I can't imagine anyone ever so much as hinting I could do something like this!"

Davis considered his next words carefully. "Your daughter implied it might not be impossible," he offered at last.

That caused the other man to sit back in his chair, his face going slack with apparent shock. "Daphne?" he all but whispered. "Daphne is here? I didn't... she didn't mention it to me, and I haven't seen her at all today."

The policeman found himself pitying this other man, who was clearly so estranged from his eldest child she did not even inform him when she was planning to be home—and had evidently been deliberately avoiding him, since even with the size of the house and the number of guests he suspected the two would have run into each other at some point otherwise.

"She is here, yes," he confirmed. "And I spoke to her a short while ago. She... did not have the kindest things to say about you."

"No, I'm sure she didn't," Trevor replied, shaking his head. "But you have to understand, we don't get along very well. And right now, she's even more angry with me than usual since I cut off her allowance a month or so back." He sighed. "I hated to do it, but she was burning through money at a prodigious rate. I'd hoped she'd learn to be more thoughtful with it, more careful, if I limited her access. The fact that she's here suggests it did not."

"I couldn't say, as to that," Davis commented. "We did not discuss finances. And certainly, I recognize that she may have a certain bias toward you. But it still introduces an element of doubt. Even setting her testimony aside as highly subjective, however, the simple facts are that you had means, motive, and opportunity. That alone is enough to charge you with her murder."

"But what about the witness?" Trevor finally managed to interject. "Surely he can confirm that I didn't do this?"

"We can't find any such person," the detective answered. "And we have only your word that they even exist." *And the opinion of one of your oldest friends that they may actually be some sort of supernatural creature,* he thought but did not add. No sense making matters worse. "You see my dilemma, I hope," he did explain instead. "You seem a decent sort, and you have been forthcoming, at least on the surface, but I have no other suspects and nothing that negates you as the prime suspect. So I don't see what else I can do here."

"Give it a little time," his host suggested, not quite begging, although there was just a tinge of desperation that crept into his voice. "It is not always easy for people to find the courage to speak to the police, even when they themselves have done nothing wrong. I'm sure you've seen that yourself." Davis nodded. He was all too familiar with such reticence, and it always made his job a good deal harder. "Hopefully, the witness's conscience will finally prick him enough that he feels compelled to speak to you. Then you'll see."

"I can perhaps allow a little more time," Davis admitted slowly. "But not too much. Murder investigations are not something we like to let linger." Though he did have several details he still hoped to ascertain, and even if they did not alter the outcome, they could at least explain a few missing pieces and puzzling elements.

"Look, I'm not going anywhere," Trevor pointed out. "You have your men at the door, anyway. Let the witness sleep on it. Most people can only rationalize inaction for so long, and it's a good deal harder to do in the cold light of morning. I'll have a room made up for you, and you can see how things look by breakfast."

The detective considered that. He also thought about what Sylvia and Doctor Halsey had said about Trevor's stubbornness and his inability to ask for help. In that light, the current request was momentous indeed — and one that was certainly within his power to grant. "I will let things stand until morning," he finally agreed. "I'll stay here, though, if that's all right with you — the couch looks comfortable enough to doze upon, and certainly I've done worse. My men will stand guard, and I'm assuming I have your word that you won't try anything in the night." Trevor nodded. "All right, then. It's settled. We'll resolve this in the morning."

"Thank you," his host said, practically leaping to his feet. "I am aware you did not have to agree, and I promise you, you will not regret such a considerate gesture. And you have my word, I'll abide by whatever decision you make then."

With that, Trevor let himself out of the room, promising as he left that he would have plates sent out to the police by the door and by the woods. Davis nodded his thanks. Once the door was shut, he attacked his own dinner, trying to set his thoughts at rest long enough to enjoy the excellent food. But he kept getting distracted by the facts of the case and barely tasted the roast beef or garlic mashed potatoes or fried clams.

Could Trevor actually be telling the truth, he kept wondering. It was possible. There could have been a witness — the story had been oddly particular for a mere fabrication. But if so, where were they? And how had they vanished, exactly? Never mind Sylvia's fanciful explanation, there had to be a more rational one; he just couldn't think of any.

And if Trevor had not killed Lisette Barnes, who had? And why? That was what had really swayed him into extending the deadline, in the end. He felt he still needed to know more about Lisette, who she was, and how she'd come to be here before he could make an informed decision. Perhaps she'd had a jealous ex-lover or a vengeful former employer who had seen her here and taken offense to the way she'd been flirting with Trevor, even if it had been at least partially one-sided. Perhaps there was something else going on, something he just couldn't see yet.

These were the things Davis knew he had to figure out, if at all possible. And he had to do it by morning, or else he would have no choice but to arrest Trevor Kinkaid and charge him with a young woman's cold-blooded murder. That still didn't feel quite right to him, and Davis had learned to trust his gut. But he'd also learned that sometimes your gut could be wrong, and that when you had no other suspects, you went with the one you did have and hoped for the best.

Chapter Eleven

It was an hour or so later, as the sun finally dipped below the horizon, stealing the pink and gold from the sky and leaving it swathed in an ever-deepening blue, that Trevor first encountered Winnie. Everyone had finished eating, and he was supervising the clearing away of the food when she slipped into the dining room.

"Ah!" At first sight of her, he startled, backing up until his hip met the table and upset one of the serving-dish covers with a mighty clatter. But he recovered himself quickly enough to give her a rueful smile. "For a second, I thought I was seeing a ghost," he explained, mopping at his brow with a pocket square. "You look enough like her, though without the bright hues." There was no need to explain who he meant.

"So I've been told," Winnie acknowledged. She studied him, a frown forming on her lips and brows as she took in his flushed cheeks and wide eyes. "Are you all right?" It seemed an odd question to ask of someone she had been investigating for several hours.

"Not particularly," he admitted with a laugh. "I'm to be arrested in the morning, for a crime I didn't commit—would you be all right, under such circumstances?"

She shook her head but, rather than offering her sympathies, boldly asked, "So you didn't kill her?"

"No, I didn't kill her!" His reply was loud enough to fill the room, and he quickly lowered his voice back to a more conversational volume as a few people glanced their way. "Of course, I didn't! Why would I?"

"She rejected you," Winnie countered bluntly.

"She did, but that's hardly a reason to hurt her, much less kill her!" Trevor shook his head. "I have been rejected before, you know. I never hurt any of them except for the occasional snide comment if their name came up later. Why would I behave any differently now?"

Winnie barely acknowledged the defense. "If you didn't kill her, who did?" she persisted.

"I don't know!" He banged his fist on the table, producing another rattle of dishes and silverware. The servants fluttered in the doorway to the kitchen, desperate to finish cleaning up and to prevent any damage but also not willing to step into the current conflict or draw their master's ire. "If I did, I wouldn't be in this mess!"

"But you said you saw the killer," Winnie reminded him bluntly. "That is what you told the detective, isn't it?"

"Yes, I saw him," her host confirmed. "But only from a distance! I was still by the house when I spied them together, and I didn't go any closer!"

She had remained by the door to the hall this whole time, but now she crossed the room in a few quick strides to confront him more closely. "Why not?" she asked, her face practically a mask, no grief or rage visible, only curiosity. "If you saw someone hurting her, why didn't you intervene?"

"He wasn't hurting her," was the answer. "Not when I saw them. They were talking, that's all. Vigorously, angrily, but still—just talking. Nothing worse."

Winnie studied him a moment longer, then seemed to reach a decision. "Show me."

"Show you? Show you what? How they were talking?" He seemed confused by the demand, which was fair given its oddity and the strange manner in which it had been delivered.

"No," she corrected. "Show me where you were when you saw them. I want to see exactly what you saw."

"What? Now?" He stared, but she did not back down, and finally, he sighed. "Fine. Come with me."

He led her down the main hall, past his study where Davis still lay as if in wait, and to a small sunroom at the back of the house. "I was in here," he explained once they'd reached the room, which was currently empty. "I was trying to get hold of myself—"

"Because you were angry," Winnie interrupted. "She'd just rejected you."

"Yes, she had," he acknowledged. "And I wasn't too happy about that—who would be? Especially when she'd seemed so... receptive to me earlier? I didn't feel like dealing with anyone just then—I couldn't stand the thought of them all eyeing me and smirking because they'd heard what had happened — so I hid in here. It's rarely occupied this time of year, it gets much too warm during the day with the sun full upon it. But I was restless, so I stepped outside instead." The sunroom's back wall was entirely windows save for the glass doors in their center, and it was these Trevor opened now, stepping out onto the back lawn. Winnie quickly followed, easing the doors shut behind her.

"I'd thought to take a turn around the yard," he said, "collect my thoughts, regain my composure, plus give the gossip a chance to die down." He winced at his unfortunate choice of words. "Then I heard something, voices, and glanced over. They were right there." He indicated the spot where, even now, a pair of policemen stood guard — Carruthers and Grant's replacements, who had taken over the post around the same time as dinner and would stay in place halfway through the night, until their own relief arrived. "Lisette and... someone. I couldn't see who. But I could see the gestures, big and angry, and hear the raised voices."

Winnie squinted across the lawn, trying to make out the officers there and imagine them as Lisette and this unknown figure instead. "And you didn't approach?"

"Why should I?" Trevor asked. "She'd just turned me down cold, after leading me on for hours! And now here she was, with some other bloke, only he wasn't too happy with her. Maybe even because he'd heard about or seen her behavior with me and didn't like the idea of his lady leading someone on. I thought that was only fair — she turns me away, he does the same to her." He sighed. "I had no idea he'd turn violent. If I had, I *would* have stepped in."

"Perhaps. Perhaps not." Winnie glanced over at him, her head cocked to one side, her gray eyes fixed on his darker ones.

"He didn't do it, you know." This time both of them started, looking around in surprise. Their eyes finally lit upon a figure leaning against the low railing surrounding the patio outside the sitting room, the red glow of her cigarette tip too dim to touch her features, though both of them recognized the sharp, knowing voice, the fine profile, the spicy smell of Habanita, and the bright, stylish dress. It was Bridget.

"How do you know for certain?" Winnie asked, focusing on the other young lady.

"I heard the detective talking," Bridget answered, rising gracefully to her feet and stepping carefully through the grass to join them. "He found tracks. Over that way."

"Tracks?" Trevor considered that. "Ah. That would be why he asked about my galoshes." He did not seem happy with this revelation but said nothing more as they all traipsed toward the corner of the house. Though growing darker, there was still enough light that Bridget, in the lead, managed to spot the footsteps from the kitchen toward the woods. She immediately pointed them out to her two companions.

"There, you see?" she declared. "The killer made those marks! And if you came from the sunroom, that couldn't have been you!"

Winnie crouched, oblivious to the risk to her dress, and studied the footprints. "They are odd," she commented, causing Trevor and Bridget to both join her.

"Oh, yes, very peculiar," Bridget offered, with the intonation of someone who has absolutely no idea what she is saying but is determined to agree anyway. But Trevor could see at once that Winnie was right. Those prints were indeed strange.

Unfortunately, he noticed something else as well. "Those are definitely from my galoshes," he said, tapping a small, undisturbed circle of dirt within one print. "There's a short, fat black nail just there in the left one's heel. I stepped on it a few years back. Decided to leave it in, it wasn't long enough to stab into me and I didn't want to risk leaving a hole in the boot by yanking it out." He rose to his feet. "Well, now I suppose Davis has the evidence he needs to bring me in."

Winnie was still studying the prints. "Why do they do that?" she wondered aloud. "It makes no sense for anyone to walk that way, their feet sliding about."

"Does it matter?" Trevor asked her. "They're my boots. It's my house — and no one else saw me in the sunroom, so I could just as easily have come from the kitchen and taken the time to pull them on along the way. She was my companion for much of the day — and I was angry with her." He scratched at his nose. "That's all they'll need."

He turned away then and made his way slowly back toward the sunroom, moving more like a man of eighty than one of not yet fifty. The two women watched him go.

"Do you think he did it?" Bridget asked once the glass doors had shut behind him.

Winnie was slow to answer, and her gaze was still on those doors. "No," she said at last. "I don't. You?"

Bridget shook her head. "Not really, no. I mean, I suppose you never know for certain, isn't that what they say? But it just seems so drastically out of character. And if he had decided to kill her, even if it was spur of the moment, why do so in the middle of a huge party—one you're throwing? That makes no sense."

Privately, Winnie agreed. That would have made no sense to her, either. But then again, she was already certain Trevor was innocent.

Unfortunately, her thoughts and opinions on the matter would hardly sway Detective Davis.

She would need a good deal more evidence to convince him to release Mister Kinkaid—that, and a whole lot more luck.

She hoped she would find it in time. And that, in doing so, she could uncover the identity of Lisette's true killer.

CHAPTER TWELVE

Meanwhile, Pat Mercer was continuing to make himself popular at others' expense. This time, his targets were none other than the recently deceased — and her more somber sister.

"What do we even really know about them?" he declared to the whole of the sitting room, many of whom continued their own conversations unabated but a fair percentage of whom did stop to listen, if only so they could mock him for it later. "This pair shows up out of nowhere, the songbird and the dove. No one knows them, they certainly don't know anyone, yet somehow they talk their way in the front door, no doubt on the strength of the fairer sister's charms." A few titters encouraged and emboldened the young man, and his voice rose in pitch and volume both. "The one seduces our poor host to her like the pied piper and some bedraggled grey-whiskered rat" — more laughs, some at Trevor's expense, though those were nervous, for it was dangerous bearding even a wounded lion in its own den — "while the other skulks in the shadows, for I certainly do not recall seeing her during the day." There was a murmur of agreement to that, at least, tinged with concern and some suspicion, for how was Winnie occupied during all that time?

"She's Lisette's shadow," one young wit opined aloud, "and thus could only be seen once the original light had been extinguished!" This was met with a smattering of applause, even as the accuracy of shadows vs. light was questioned by a few others behind their hands and with many a knowing glance. Still, Mercer seized on the theme.

"Indeed, just so!" he declared, throwing his arms wide as if he were an actor upon the stage. "So the one flutters, the other lurks. The one shines, the other glowers." He grinned at his own audacity before taking a deep breath and plunging to the heart of the matter. "And then — the one dies!"

The entire room went silent, shocked. It was the height of bad manners to discuss such a thing, and so openly, with such enthusiasm! Yet that very impropriety was what had his audience laughing along with him, egging him on, daring him to go even farther.

"Yes, she dies!" Mercer continued gleefully. "And not by random mishap, either. She is murdered! Right here on these very grounds! And where, pray tell, is her shadow sister when it occurs? No one knows! But after the fair Lisette perishes, oh, then suddenly we cannot seem to be rid of her darker twin! Everywhere we turn, there she is, staring with those soft, murky eyes, smiling with that little smirk, and always asking questions! Where were you when it happened? What were you doing at the time? Was anyone else about who could confirm you were there? As if she had somehow transformed into an officer of the law!"

He paused then, to smirk himself, and continued in a dramatic aside, "Though it's not as if they're doing much good either, are they?"

The laughter was nervous again. It was one thing to slight some unfortunate young woman, or even her tragically murdered sister, quite another to taunt their host — and even farther to mock the sharp-eyed detective still residing somewhere in their midst, who had the power to haul any one of them off in chains.

Sensing that he was near to losing his listeners' support, Mercer quickly stumbled back to more solid ground. "He has questioned many of us, this detective, has he not?" he asked. "But perhaps the one he should be questioning — is her! The sister who lived in her twin's shadow, no doubt envying her light and warmth! The same sister we didn't see until after her brighter half was dead! Maybe she's the one who should be divulging her whereabouts and naming witnesses to support her own innocence!"

Though no doubt shocked by his daring, this accusation was indeed one the crowd was more comfortable with than attacking a policeman. Nor was the theory completely without merit. Still, if he'd hoped anyone would act upon such a suspicion, Mercer was swiftly disappointed, for no one showed any interest in leaping to their feet and seeking out the young lady in question. Instead, after smiles and nods and a few polite claps, they all returned to their drinks and their chatter about the weather and the club's newly refinished tennis courts.

"Quite the energetic assault on someone you barely know," someone commented, and Mercer turned to find Bridget studying him from the doorway to the patio. "Is there some reason in particular you dislike her? Or are you simply keen to make sure all attention is turned elsewhere—perhaps because you fear any of it tilting back your way?"

He glared at her, their rivalry once more unleashed. "What are you insinuating?" he demanded hotly. "Best be careful, or you'll find yourself sued for public defamation of character." It was one of the few legal phrases he had bothered to learn, and something he trotted out whenever he wished to appear more learned about the law.

The threat slid harmlessly off Bridget, however—she merely laughed it away. "If I called you a lecherous little slime who would do or say anything to gain attention and had no morals, no backbone, and no redeeming qualities," she stated brightly, to many a snicker, "that would be public defamation of character, dear boy. As it is"—and she hit him with a smile bright as the noonday sun and sharp as a shard of glass—"I've said no such thing, only wondered if your attempts to pin something on Winnie might actually be an attempt at deflection. Those two statements are hardly in the same league, don't you agree?"

The laughter was significantly louder than during Mercer's earlier diatribe, and all aimed at him but as its target rather than its patron. The young man's face turned red under such heat, and he growled but did not otherwise reply, choosing instead to gather his tattered pride about him like an old cloak and slink quickly from the room.

"What a bore," Bridget stated to no one in particular—and then turned to glance over her shoulder at the woman who had not yet entered the room but had instead stayed in the shadows outside. "I wouldn't worry overmuch about him. No one takes him seriously."

Winnie nodded and stepped inside, but her eyes followed Mercer's exit, and her mouth was pursed in a thin, tight line that suggested a good deal of concern, and some anger as well. She excused herself a few minutes later under the pretext of freshening her makeup and glided across the room, her footsteps all but soundless on the handsome carpet, to vanish into the hall beyond.

Her departure was well-timed, for mere moments later, Mercer himself returned. He did not approach anyone directly, however. Instead, he drew himself up to his full height there in the doorway and cleared his throat. "I have something I must say," he declared loudly, as all eyes turned toward him. "And it is this—Monica Gardner and Lawrence Todd are having an affair!"

The room filled with gasps. The pair in question had been sitting beside one another on the settee before the fireplace, but with this pronouncement, both leapt to their feet and started guiltily apart. Monica burst into tears and ran from the room, shoving past the smirking Mercer as she went. Todd, his face red with rage, started toward the other young man in a rush but never reached him, for Mercer turned and fled even as Will and a few others laid hold of Todd to prevent him from doing anything foolish with police all around the house. A few of the women went after Monica to comfort her as well.

The entire room was abuzz, of course. Not out of shock at the discovery, for it was a fact well known within their small community. Monica was the victim of an unhappy marriage to a man many years her senior, her late first husband's former business partner who had assumed all his old friend's debts in exchange for her hand. Fortunately, the man seemed more interested in having Monica on his arm at formal dinners than in otherwise consummating the marriage, and she was free to pursue what happiness she could find, provided she was discreet. She had found in Todd a kind and considerate partner, and one who was more than willing to be circumspect, and the rest of their circle were happy to uphold the fiction that the two were merely friends. It was only Mercer's open announcement that had upset everyone by forcing them all to acknowledge that which they had all tacitly ignored before. It was fortunate that Monica's husband had been forced to beg off attending tonight, as he had been called away on urgent business, which had prevented an utter disaster.

Once Todd had been returned to a state of calm or at least talked down from a murderous rage, and Monica had been soothed and coaxed back out from the powder room and reunited with her paramour under absolute assurances from all that the entire assemblage had evidently fallen inexplicably deaf for the space of two minutes surrounding that strange and utterly preposterous accusation, a small party was formed. It consisted of Winthrop, Bridget—the two united past their usual rivalry for once—Lowder, and a handful of others. The group of them went searching through the house and shortly found their quarry sulking in one of the secondary studies.

"What do you want?" Mercer demanded as they all entered, arraying themselves around the room and facing him like some disconcertingly gaily attired jury. "Come to gloat? Yes, it was an excellent comeuppance, points to you. Happy?"

"Not nearly, but getting there," Bridget replied sharply, then shifted and offered Winthrop the speaker's role. His nod of thanks was more polite than the two of them typically were, and all the more for its apparent authenticity. His pleasant demeanor vanished, however, as he turned to face Mercer, all geniality melting away to be replaced, not with smarm and charm for once, but with a hard, fierce rage that gave the young man surprising dignity.

"Patrick Thomas Mercer," he stated, his words echoing in the small, wood-paneled room, each syllable striking their subject like a blow. "You are hereby cast out." That said, Winthrop turned away and began to leave, along with the others.

"Cast out?" Mercer bleated, rising to his feet in alarm. "What do you mean? Why?"

"You know why," Bridget snapped. "And as to what it means, surely your nearly legal mind can parse it? You're no longer one of us, you silly little man. We want nothing more to do with you. Any of us." She waved him away like a bit of errant dust. "You are not welcome here any longer."

"You can't leave, of course," Will pointed out helpfully. "Not with the police and all." His face hardened as well, unusually so for such a normally sunny young man, but then he was friends with Todd and quite liked and had always felt for Monica. "But stay away from the rest of us. For good."

"This is ridiculous," Mercer sputtered. "You can't mean this! All for that? I didn't say anything everyone wasn't already thinking!"

"Perhaps not, but you were the one who said it," Winthrop pointed out, reaching the door and holding it open for the others. "And that is unforgivable."

They exited then, shutting the door behind them and leaving Mercer to wallow in his new exile. He did not attempt to follow them out—and so he never saw the dove-gray young lady in the hall, or the faint but undeniable smirk on her mild features as she watched the jury walk away, having delivered their fatal sentence.

CHAPTER THIRTEEN

Davis did not see any of this little drama play out, for he was engaged on another mission. He had set himself the task of figuring out exactly how Lisette had first arrived at the party, and so found himself asking that question of whole groups at a time to speed up the process.

Luck was with him in this, for he was only on his third repetition of the question when from that particular cluster a young man started.

"Oh," he said, glancing about him a little guiltily. "That—I think that would be me, actually."

The detective quickly spirited the young man, who was of average height and build and decent but not particularly overwhelming appearance but did possess very thick and glossy chestnut hair and very strong white teeth, away to the study to question him privately.

Once there, he wasted no time finding out the young man's name—Randall Sawyer—and asking how exactly he had known Lisette Barnes.

"Um, well, I didn't, not really," Sawyer replied, tugging at his collar. "I mean, I did tell her about the party and that she should come. But I didn't really know her."

Davis, who had returned to his customary seat behind the desk, frowned at the young man. "Are you in the habit, then, of inviting strangers to parties?" He allowed some sternness to creep into both voice and gaze and was pleased to see his companion grow more flustered.

"No!" Sawyer answered quickly. "I mean, not exactly!" He sighed. "Look, you saw her, right?" A smile spread unbidden across his face. "She was lovely! And, well, not to put too fine a point on things, but she was clearly one of us, wasn't she?" It was obvious from the way he said that last that he was not, in fact, including the detective, but rather the rest of the partygoers. "We met at Tafnee's, you know it?" Davis nodded. It was a café and quite an elegant one, the sort of place he would never go unless invited to a specific event or if he were desperately trying to impress someone, as a single meal there could cost an entire paycheck. But of course, it was exactly where someone like Sawyer might go without thinking twice. "Well, I was there with a few others," the young man continued, his trepidation fading as he lost himself in reminiscences, "and Lisette was there, pretty as a peach. We got to talking, she mentioned that she was new in town and didn't really know anyone, and I told her, 'I've just the thing, old Trevor Kinkaid's having one of his shindigs this weekend, everyone who's anyone'll be there, you've got to come!' She demurred at first, said that wouldn't be right, they'd never met, but I assured her it was fine, people brought friends and relatives all the time. Told her she could just tell him I'd invited her." He looked very pleased with himself over that, then the smile fell away as he recalled the result of that particular invitation. "Oh."

Davis nodded, but without the same sharpness as before. After all, how could anyone have known where such an innocent and seemingly generous offer would lead? "Did you see her here today?" he asked instead. "Did you meet up with her and escort her in?"

"Yes—no," the other man answered, then hurried to explain. "I mean, yes, I saw her, but she was already walking about with Trevor by then, and I wasn't about to get in the middle of that! I didn't bring her, though. Just told her the address and time. She thanked me very prettily and said she'd hope to see me there."

"I see. Is there anything else you can tell me?" Davis asked. "That day at Tafnee's, was she with anyone? Did she tell you where she was from? Or anything else about herself?"

Sawyer frowned, clearly trying to recall. "She wasn't with anyone," he said finally, dredging his memories. "She was in the entryway, actually, when I saw her. She looked as if she were waiting for someone to meet her there. We were just heading in and I stopped to chat her up a bit, but then—you know, I don't recall seeing her seated anywhere afterward. Huh." He shook his head. "As to the rest—no, not really. We just exchanged pleasantries, you know, the usual. She said she was from out of town but not where exactly." He seemed surprised by his own sheer lack of knowledge, but Davis discovered he was not. Something about the remembered conversation had already struck him as, not cagey exactly but restrained, carefully orchestrated. He had no doubt, picturing the scene in his head, that Lisette had not in fact been meeting anyone at Tafnee's but had instead been laying in wait for just such a young man as Randall Sawyer, someone who would be swayed by her bright eyes and pretty smile. But to what end? To gain an invite to the party? Or, more generally, an entrée into this world?

Sawyer seemed to have no further information, and so Davis dismissed him, rising himself and following the young man out. He continued on down the hall, past the dining room, to the front doors, where two of his officers, Mead and Baker, were stationed. Both men straightened to attention when he stepped outside to join them.

"All quiet?" he asked, and both nodded. The air had grown pleasantly crisp now that night had fully arrived, and the stars sparkled overhead. "Do you have that list of cars?" Mead handed it over at once. Davis had given the police at the front door three tasks: don't let anyone leave, don't let anyone new enter, and compile a list of the cars in the drive and who owned them. He checked the list now, but Lisette's name was not on it, nor was Winnie's, for that matter. So they had not driven here, or at least not driven themselves. Could they have induced someone to give them a ride? Unlikely, since the only person here he was sure either had met before today was Sawyer, and he had not brought them. But in that case, how had they gotten here?

Returning inside, he stepped over to the nearest phone and quickly dialed the station. Carruthers answered, as Davis had half-expected— he knew the uniformed officer well enough to know he'd head back to his desk for at least a short time before going home, even at this hour.

"Carruthers, it's me," Davis said quickly. "Listen, do you know if anyone was able to get hold of the taxi companies?" He'd put in a request to check with all the local taxi services and find out which guests, if any, had taken cabs here.

"Aye, Connelly did," Carruthers answered. "Hang on, I'll get it from him." He was back a moment later and answered before Davis could even ask, "our girl's not on here."

"Damn. All right. Thanks." Davis sighed. Of course, that would have been too easy! "Anything from Doc Peterson?"

"No, sir. I can have him give you a ring, though."

"Please. Thanks." Davis hung up and brooded a second. So Lisette hadn't driven and hadn't hired a taxi. How did she get here, then? Had she driven and left her car out of sight, perhaps because it didn't match up to all the shiny, expensive convertibles that lined the drive? That would make sense.

Coming to a quick decision, he exited the house again, nodding to the two officers. "I'll be back shortly," he called as he hurried down the drive to his own sedan, which was parked along the curb. Settling into the driver's seat, he fired up the engine and pulled away, but slowly. It was late enough that most people were already home for the night, and there was very little traffic, especially out here. If Lisette had parked nearby, he should be able to spot the car easily enough.

He drove slowly, scanning the sides of the road as best he could, for there were no streetlights and his own headlamps only illuminated so much. The nearest house was a good fifteen minutes away, and he saw no stray cars in all that time. Damn! How had she gotten here, then? Walked? If that was the case, he'd never find out where she'd come from!

He went a bit farther, far enough that the houses became a bit closer together, and both smaller and more pedestrian. Sidewalks sprang up, and streetlights, and now he was in a proper neighborhood instead of the grounds of a grand home. Still, that didn't help him any.

He was about to give up and turn back when his headlights reflected off something up ahead, right along the curb. Something tall and thin and metallic, and widening out at the top. A bus sign.

That was curious. There weren't a lot of bus stops out here. Still, he pulled up alongside it and jotted down the bus number, then hopped out, leaving the car idling, and examined the posted schedule as best he could. The next bus was due in — he checked his watch — five minutes. Well, it was worth a shot. Pulling a bit farther forward to get out of the bus's spot, Davis shut off the engine, exited the car, and returned to the sign to wait.

Sure enough, five minutes later, the bus pulled up. There wasn't anyone on it except a pair of older women toward the back, and so Davis did not feel too bad about hopping inside and showing the driver his badge. "How long have you been on today?" he asked the man, who looked to be around Trevor's age but a good bit shorter and thicker, with far less hair up top but a bushy mustache to compensate.

"Since noon," the bus driver answered. "And this is my last go-round for the night, so if you don't mind?"

"I'm trying to track down a girl," Davis countered. "She might've got off here earlier today. Young, early to mid-twenties. Pretty. Blonde. Blue eyes. Pale blue dress."

The driver grinned, making his mustache twitch. "Oh, aye, I remember her! Who could forget, a looker like that?" He winked at Davis. "She need to get picked up again? Her I'd wait for!"

The detective resisted the retort that rose to his lips. "Can you tell me anything else about her?" he asked, forcing himself not to snap. "Where she got on? If she was alone?"

"Oh, she was alone, right enough," the driver answered. "Where she got on? Sure. Downtown." He named the exact stop, which was near the heart of downtown. Not a residential area, nor a high-toned one, but not dangerously destitute, either. Now the older man frowned. "Everything all right? She cause some kind of trouble? She was quiet enough on the bus. Smiled and said thank you when she got on and when she got off."

"No, no trouble," Davis answered. "Thank you." He stepped back down and let the bus continue on its way, returning to his car and retracing his steps to the Kinkaid house. So Lisette had taken the bus as close as she could and then had walked. Interesting. That suggested someone who couldn't afford a car or a taxi and didn't want anyone to know it. And where had her sister been? Why had they arrived separately?

He had just reached the front steps when Mead saw him and beckoned him over. "Got the doc on the phone for you," the officer explained, gesturing inside. "He just rang."

Davis thanked him and hurried past, grabbing up the phone. "Doc? Sorry, I'm here."

"Good, good," the medical examiner replied. "You wanted an update? I've finished the autopsy. Death by strangulation, as expected. I'm not seeing any traces of anything in her system, though I'll have to run a full tox screen to be sure. No defensive wounds, and no fingerprints, either—whoever killed her was wearing gloves at the time. Not rough ones, either—linen or silk or fine leather, something along those lines. No blood under her nails, so she didn't manage to get in any scratches, more's the pity." Davis knew that was said half out of sympathy for a young woman whose life had been unfairly cut short and half because blood would have made their job a good deal easier.

There was the next question, which Davis hated to ask but knew he had to. "Any sign of intercourse?"

"No, at least nothing recent," the doctor answered. "Not a virgin, but certainly nothing in the past few days. Beyond that, couldn't say."

Davis let out a breath. So she hadn't been sexually assaulted, at least. Nor had she slept with Trevor. Either would have been bad news for the older gentleman.

"That's all I've got for now," Peterson concluded, but Davis had a question for him.

"How are her hands?" he asked.

"Hm? No blood, like I said."

"That's not what I mean," the detective explained. "Does she have any calluses, rough skin, anything like that?"

"Ah, I see what you're asking. Hold on." There was a muted clatter as the phone was set down, and a few minutes later, it was picked back up again. "Yes, now that you mention it, she does. I'd say she'd done some work, nothing major but shelving, secretarial, mild factory, something. Not the hands of a lady."

"Thanks." Davis had the doctor transfer him back to Carruthers, who he asked to follow up on a few more things based on what he'd just learned. Then he hung up and considered what he knew. Lisette had not been "one of them," as Sawyer had thought. She'd just made herself look and sound the part. Why? Just to step into the good life? Maybe to find a rich husband? Plenty of people had done the same, and nothing particularly wrong with that. Still, if someone had found out she was a sham, could that be why they'd killed her? How would Trevor have reacted if he'd learned that his new favorite was no more than a poor factory worker, no better than one of the maids, putting on airs? Would that have been enough of an affront to make him lose his temper, hit her, throttle her, lose control and kill her?

Acting on a hunch, Davis headed through the dining room and into the kitchen, ignoring the few staff still there as he continued on to the portico. Hanging on the hook over where the boots had been was a large, handsome overcoat, no doubt also Trevor's. He checked the inside collar — sure enough, "Property of Trevor Kinkaid" had been sewn in there. Next, Davis searched the coat's pockets. Tucked into the front left was a pair of fine kid gloves.

That didn't prove anything, of course. But it was another potential nail in the host's coffin.

Even so, Davis decided to wait a little longer and see what developed. He'd promised the older man he'd give him until morning, after all. And he was a man of his word.

CHAPTER FOURTEEN

An encounter took place in the hall, which was uncharacteristically empty given the number of people currently confined to the house. Two women, one in dove-gray still — under normal circumstances, there would have been titters about only having brought one outfit to a party! — and the other clad in a delicate rose that tried desperately to counter the strident line of her jaw. It was the latter who spied the former flitting through the empty space and, hurrying over, stopped her with an outstretched hand, saying, "You are the sister of that poor girl, are you not?"

Winnie dipped her head in mute acknowledgment, then peered through long, dark lashes that needed no embellishment up at her smartly dressed accoster. "And you are Daphne Kinkaid, I believe?" Her words were as soft as ever, though there might have been a pointed jab hidden well within them.

"I am." Daphne nodded curtly before barreling on. "I just wanted to tell you how sorry I am about your sister. I feel terrible. That my own father could do such a thing!" She rested one pink-gloved hand against her forehead, the very picture of contrition and grief.

"Thank you." If Winnie's own voice was less fraught with anguish, less throbbing with emotion, her eyes were steady and sad, whereas Daphne's own gaze might be said to be, at best, impenetrable and, at worst, calculating. "So you think your father killed her, then?"

Evidently, the question was unexpected enough to make the mistress of the house lower her arm and regard the smaller woman with some surprise. "Well, yes — isn't it obvious?" She tutted, tapping a finger against her expertly painted lower lip. "Father has, I regret to say, always had a temper. He keeps it in check much of the time, of course, but he can't abide being crossed—or rejected. It brings out the worst in him."

"One could say that about almost anyone," Winnie argued, though not hotly. "There is a long, long ways to go, however, from being at your worst and committing murder. Especially by so violent an act as strangling."

"Hm, true, but—well, let's just say I have seen him behave in similar ways, if less final ones." The taller woman rubbed her arms as if suddenly chilled. "As I said, he has always had a temper."

"Odd that no one else has commented on that being the case, then." Winnie was studying her hostess closely as she said that and did not miss the way her face tightened, her jaw clenching and her brow furrowing for an instant before she regained control.

"Well, no one else here knows him the way I do," Daphne snapped. "Obviously." She straightened to her full height, towering over the smaller Winnie. "I'm sorry if you're offended on his behalf. I am only trying to do right by your sister."

"If the killer is brought to justice, that will be enough," Winnie replied, undaunted by the difference in their height. "But only if it truly is the person responsible." Her calm gaze met Daphne's irate one. "And I am not convinced your father is that person."

"Who else, then?" Came the furious reply. "Who else would have reason, much less opportunity? He spent the whole day chasing after her, she rejected him, he went after her, they argued, he lost his temper and killed her! Plain and simple!" She said that with the air of one very used to having her own way, the words crisp and clear like a case snapping shut.

But her audience of one was still not swayed. "As for opportunity, anyone at the party might have seen her out there on the lawn and confronted her alone," Winnie argued, her words still unhurried and tinged more with consideration than any strong emotion. "And for reason, who can say? Perhaps someone she already knew before the party. Perhaps someone who took offense at seeing your father with her. Perhaps someone who did not like the way he was pursuing her—or the way she had spurned him." Her gaze sharpened, spearing the taller woman. "You must not have appreciated either of those, seeing your father chasing after a woman roughly your own age and then seeing him rejected. Loyalty to your dead mother warring with pride in your father? Where were *you* when all this took place?"

"What? Don't be preposterous!" Daphne snarled, leaning in to thrust her face close to Winnie's in an attempt to stare her down, her rich perfume wafting over the other woman like an expensive, almost cloying cloud. "I was here, with everyone else, of course! I'm not the one you should be questioning! Go demand of my father where he was and what he was doing!"

"I've already spoken to him," came the calm response. "He was a good deal less incensed at being questioned than you are now. And yet you say he is the one with the temper?" The jab was less concealed now, and made the taller woman recoil, her face paling and then flushing to a shade darker than her attire.

"How dare you!" A gloved hand was raised, as if to slap, but just as quickly lowered. Instead, Daphne turned sharply and stomped from the room, the clack of her heels on the ground oddly uneven, a broken rhythm that had Winnie studying the other woman's retreat. Curious, that.

"Hoy!' Officer Wilkins called, straightening at the sound of approaching footsteps and the vague sight of a dark shape silhouetted against the lights of the house. "Who goes there?"

Beside him, Officer Holden shone the beam of his flashlight forward, playing it across the lawn until it lit upon a figure in a plain dark suit. He shifted his grip to raise the light higher, finally landing it on the man's face, which was clean and somber—and very familiar.

"Oh, sorry, sir!" Wilkins said, nodding as his partner lowered the light from their superior's face. "Didn't expect you, this hour." They had taken over for Carruthers and Grant only a few hours before. "All's quiet here, though."

"Good, good," Davis replied, stepping a bit closer but stopping well shy of the crime scene. "Just checking in a bit." He glanced around him, studying his surroundings, and then seemed to spot something, striding a few paces away before sinking into a crouch.

"Problem, sir?" Holden joined him there and helpfully shone the flashlight on the spot the detective was studying. In that light, the footprints stood out cleanly. "Oh, right."

Davis didn't say anything but reached out and traced the outline of one print, his fingers not quite touching the flattened grass and imprinted dirt.

"Bit funny, isn't it?" the officer tried again. "Should be sharper around the edges, right? Looks a little slippery, almost—like my tire tracks when I'm caught in snow and can't get proper traction."

The detective glanced his way at that, and Holden frowned. He'd been certain his superior's eyes were a good deal darker than his own, but in the night-time shadows, they looked lighter, almost more gray than brown. Still, the man's voice was the same as he said, "That is an excellent point. Thank you."

"Uh—of course, sir. Happy to help." Davis stood, and so Holden did as well, quickly backpedaling so they wouldn't collide. "Did you need anything else, sir?"

"No, thank you." The detective nodded at him and Wilkins. "Carry on." Then he turned and made his way back toward the house at a determined pace that quickly carried him from view as the shadows swallowed him back up.

"Strange," Wilkins said as his partner rejoined him. "He ain't usually so brusque."

"No," Holden agreed. He considered mentioning the thing about the eyes but then shook it off. Surely it had just been some trick of the light, and he'd sound an idiot if he said anything! "Guess he's just worried about the case, is all."

That was something they could at least agree on, for everyone knew Detective Davis took murders quite seriously and very much to heart. It was part of what made him such a good detective, that he truly seemed to empathize with the victims. And if that meant he was less chatty than usual, what of it? Neither officer took offense. The man was just doing his job, after all, and doing it well. That was what mattered.

A short while later, Davis was startled by a knock on the study door. After speaking to Carruthers once more, he had been half-dozing on the couch and sat up sharply at the sound, scrambling to his feet and stumbling toward the door, shaking off sleep as he went. "Yes?" he asked even as he tugged the door open—and found himself faced with a familiar young lady in soft grey. "Miss... Barnes? What can I do for you at this hour?"

"I need to ask you about something." Winnie did not wait for an invitation but slipped under his arm and into the room, spinning to face him as she did. "You have Mister Kinkaid's galoshes, is that correct?"

"I—" Davis shut the door again and turned, placing his back against the comforting wood. "Yes. I do." There seemed no reason to deny it—at least half the house was already aware of the fact.

"I'd like to see them, if I may." Her gentle but clear gaze was already sweeping the room and soon alighted upon the objects in question, laying on their sides on the floor by the desk. She hurried over, crouching and reaching, but stopped before her hands could brush the pliable rubber. "May I?"

Davis frowned, crossing to join her as he considered. On the one hand, he was normally a stickler for rules, especially the sanctity of any collected evidence. On the other, this case was already an unusual one, including the fact that he was spending the night at the scene of the crime, and the young lady was not only clearly committed to getting justice for the deceased but also startlingly perceptive. Plus, there was little she could do to disturb the galoshes or invalidate their role at this point, particularly with him watching. "Go ahead," he finally decided.

She picked up the nearest boot and brought it in for closer inspection. But, much to the detective's surprise, she did not flip it over to study the mud caked to its soles. Instead, she raised the boot to her face and, leaning over the opening, took a deep, thorough sniff. Strange!

The small smile that touched her lips suggested she had gained something from the experience, however. And so Davis was not entirely unprepared when she twisted to face him and extended the same boot. "Now you," she instructed. "Take a good whiff."

Though that would hardly be the strangest thing he'd ever done in the course of an investigation, Davis hesitated even as his hands reflexively accepted the footwear. "Why?" he asked, studying not the boot but the young lady who'd handed it to him.

"You'll understand once you do," she replied with a smug little grin. "But I don't want to prejudice you beforehand. Just smell, and you'll see."

Deciding he had little to lose, Davis finally did as suggested, lowering his face until his nose was practically buried in the boot and then inhaling strongly. His eyes widened as the smell filled his head, and he glanced up to meet Winnie's smirk. "Is that—?"

"It is," she answered. "And I believe we now know the answer to another question, too." She nodded at the boot and, more precisely, at its sole.

Davis considered that, lowering the item back to the floor. Yes, that made sense and caused certain other details to slot into place as well. He rose to his feet and offered Winnie a hand up, which she accepted. "I take it you have an idea on how to proceed?" he asked her once they were both upright and facing each other.

"I do." She smiled at him as she disengaged and took a step away. "If you are willing to follow my lead."

This time it was he who grinned, just before he swept into a reasonably grandiose bow. "By all means—lead on."

CHAPTER FIFTEEN

Another hallway encounter. The corridor once again oddly quiet, almost as if arranged to be so. The same two women, dove-gray and soft rose, the one smelling of pine and cloves and the other of vanilla and bergamot. This time, however, it was the former who sought the latter and approached her.

"Miss Kinkaid," Winnie called, and the lady of the house stopped and turned.

"Yes?" That single word held enough chill for a thousand sherbets.

"I'm sorry." Winnie cast her eyes downward, peering up only through her lashes. "I just wanted to say that. I was unkind before, not to mention inappropriate. I was simply distraught about Lisette, as you must be about your father."

"Yes." There was some thawing evident in the repetition. "Well." And now Daphne reached out, resting a gloved hand on the smaller woman's cheek, just above the wispy gray scarf knotted loosely around her neck. "Of course, dear. Who could blame you? Such an awful thing. I forgive you, of course. Thank you."

"Thank you." Winnie proffered a timid smile, which seemed to melt the last of her hostess's resentment. "How are you coping? Is there anything I can do?"

"Oh, that's very sweet of you," she was told, "but no, I imagine I will manage." Daphne glanced around them and could not prevent a smug little smile from appearing briefly as she took in the handsome parquet floor, the fine woodwork detailing the walls and doors, the elegant paintings and sculptures and flower arrangements lining the walls, the crystal chandelier glittering high above. "Yes, I shall manage."

She started to turn away, but Winnie persisted in the conversation. "Do you have somewhere to go?" she asked, arresting the taller woman's departure instantly. "That is, if not... not to presume, but I could certainly recommend... I mean..."

The look she received in reply was half-puzzlement, half-annoyance, and tinged with a hint of triumph that was suddenly held at bay. "Whatever do you mean, dear?" Daphne asked. "I will be here, of course. Someone will need to take charge of all this with my father... well, indisposed."

"Oh, until the trial, of course," the smaller woman agreed. "Once they hand down the verdict, though... and I'm sorry, but I can't imagine that will take long. As you said, it seems obvious enough what happened."

Now she had her companion's full attention as Daphne folded silk-gloved arms across her chest. "I'm afraid I don't follow you," she admitted frankly, any pretense set aside for the moment. "Why should the verdict make any difference?"

Winnie blinked up at her. "Oh, I'm sorry!" Her own hands flew to her mouth, her gray eyes going wide. "I thought you knew!"

A single stride brought the other woman closer, though not without a quick wince. "Knew what?" she demanded, reaching out and taking Winnie by the shoulders in a strong, almost bruising grip. "What are you talking about?"

"Your father's possessions," the smaller woman was able to gasp out, leaning back slightly from both Miss Kinkaid's fierce gaze and from the cloud of scent that enveloped her. "If convicted, it all becomes forfeit."

"What?!?" The grip tightened painfully. "Impossible!"

"I'm afraid not," Winnie explained in almost a whimper. "It's the law—if you're convicted of murder, the state claims all that you own. It will sell everything off and use part of that money to defray any costs of the trial." She glanced away before adding, "Some may be awarded as damages to the family of the deceased, as well."

"No!" Daphne shook her hard. "They're going to take my house, my money, everything?" It was difficult to tell if Winnie's nod was from the jostling or out of affirmation. "That's—no! I won't have it!" She released the poor girl and stepped away, slamming her fists against her own sides. "Absolutely not! After all this, to lose everything—I won't stand for it!"

"I'm sorry." Winnie straightened her dress where it had been rumpled. "I thought you knew." She darted a quick, shy glance at her recent aggressor. "If I... that is to say, if the court decides... well, I hope you know you'll be welcome here as long as you like."

That brought her the full attention of the other woman again, and far angrier than before. "What are you saying, you little guttersnipe?" Daphne demanded, once again thrusting her face close enough to brush Winnie's nose with the tip of her own. "You'd let me stay here? You think the court would award *you* this house? Why, because your sister died here? Never!" Those big, strong hands clamped down again, squeezing hard, and Winnie found herself being tossed about like in a storm. "You think I'd let you sully this place with your lowborn touch? I wouldn't let your sister taint it, why would I let you instead?"

"My... sister...?" Winnie managed to gasp out despite the tumult. "You..."

"Yes, me!" Daphne sneered. "You think I'd let that trash seduce my father into giving her a place here? Not a chance! She didn't belong in this house—and neither do you!" She released her hold on Winnie, but only to raise her hands higher and contract the gap between them, shifting from the other woman's shoulders—to her throat. "Now you can die just like she did!" The lady of the house snarled, her fingers tightening and cutting off her victim's air.

Winnie blinked up at her, startled—and then almost seemed to wink. All of a sudden, Daphne let out a cry and stumbled backward, hands jerking convulsively away from the other woman's neck. The palms and fingertips of her pale gloves were torn in places and seeping blood.

Davis emerged from the shadows of a nearby doorway in time to catch the lady of the house as she wobbled, his own grip firm but far less punishing. "Daphne Kinkaid," he declared, moving his hands to her wrists and drawing them behind her, "you are under arrest for the murder of Lisette Barnes." He tugged a pair of handcuffs from his jacket pocket and clamped them down, first one and then the other. Only after he'd made sure the murderess was properly restrained did he examine the blood staining her gloves. "Nasty wounds, those."

Winnie had drifted closer, though carefully stopping just out of reach. Now she smiled and tugged her scarf down, revealing a choker that glittered with sharply cut stones. "The advantage of a well-chosen accessory," she said drily. "It can save your life."

"Indeed." Davis frowned, for he had not noticed the jewelry before and prided himself on spotting details, but of course, she must have changed accessories just prior to her little performance, and the scarf had neatly concealed the adjustment from view.

Meanwhile, his captive sneered. "You can't prove anything," she claimed. "Everything points to my father."

"Oh, you did a thorough job," the detective agreed, taking her bound wrists in one hand and applying enough pressure to start her walking with her odd gait down the hall, toward the front door. "Putting on his galoshes was an especially nice touch."

"A shame that was your undoing," Winnie added from where she followed close behind. Guests began to peer out from doorways, alerted by the noise of the confrontation, whispering amongst themselves as they saw who was in custody.

Daphne stiffened, and both of them noticed. "Yes," Davis agreed, though he was normally more close-lipped about the details in a case. Still, he kept his voice pitched low enough that none of the onlookers would be able to overhear. "We notice you're stepping a little awkwardly, Miss Kinkaid. Blisters, is it? That can happen when you try walking in boots that're too big for you. It's also why the footprints were so strange—your feet kept sliding around inside your father's galoshes."

"You can't prove that," the young woman hissed, though her shoulders had slumped a little at the new information.

"Ah, but I can," Davis corrected, halting her with a quick tug and stepping around as they reached the door so that he could grasp the handle and tug it open. "You see, you were smart to switch to his boots from your own shoes and to pull on his overcoat. What you forgot was, you're wearing a very expensive perfume. Guerlain Shalimar, I believe?" He sniffed and smiled. "The same scent currently wafting from both the galoshes and the overcoat. Not something your father would wear, obviously, and I've yet to notice anyone else here at the party with it." Mead and Baker had turned as the door slid wide. "Please escort Miss Kinkaid to the station," Davis instructed at a more normal volume, causing a fresh wave of conversation from those guests nearby. His officers showed no surprise themselves and quickly stepped to either side of the young lady in question, each one taking an arm. "Book her for first-degree murder. I'll be along shortly to write up the report." The policemen nodded and headed off, half-dragging the struggling, cursing woman between them.

The detective shut the door and glanced over at Winnie, who was still only a few paces behind him. Then he tipped an imaginary hat, and she smiled and dipped into a quick, graceful curtsey before stepping back and letting the growing crowd swallow her up.

CHAPTER SIXTEEN

Davis had planned to seek out his host next, to explain what had just happened, but there was no need — the gossip traveled far faster than he could have, and he had only taken a handful of steps from the door when Trevor burst through the crowd to confront him. The man looked both shocked and relieved, and before he could utter a word Davis gestured to follow him and led the way to the study for the last time.

The older man was smart enough to follow such instructions, and it was only once they were both safely within the study and the heavy doors had slid shut that he asked, "Daphne killed her? Really?"

"It does appear so, yes," the detective replied. He had let his feet lead him back to the desk out of habit but now turned and deliberately leaned against its front edge instead, putting him and his host on more equal footing. "I'm very sorry, sir. It seems she engineered the event to place blame on you so that she could gain control of your household and your accounts."

That staggered the other man, who turned and poured himself a stiff drink, setting his coffee mug aside for once in favor of a more conventional tumbler. After downing the whiskey, he crossed the room to sink into one of the armchairs. "I never..." he muttered, then stopped and visibly composed himself. "Thank you, detective," he began again. "It's true that Daphne has always been focused on material possessions, money and what it can buy for her. I cut her off a month or so back — did I tell you that already? I did. I'm sorry." He rubbed a hand over his face. "I don't even know what I'm saying anymore. I know she was upset, but to do something like this..."

"Yes, well..." Davis stuck his hands in his pockets, hating this part as always. It was nearly as difficult dealing with the shock of a killer's family, coming to terms with what their loved one had done, as it was comforting the family of the victim, stricken by their loss. "I don't think she intended anything of the sort when she arrived today, if that helps any. I believe what happened was this — she came to beg you to reinstate her allowance, only to see you walking about with Miss Barnes. Your interest was plain to all, and she must have worried that, if you and the young lady did enter into a relationship, her chances of inheriting would be significantly reduced. She decided to confront the object of your affections — it's entirely possible she didn't even know that your efforts had been rejected."

Trevor frowned, staring off into space. "So Daphne tried to warn her off? Why wouldn't Lisette have just said she wasn't interested anyway and been done with it?"

"She may have," the detective admitted. "But that wasn't enough. Especially once your daughter realized something." That brought the other man's gaze into focus on him. "Lisette Barnes did not come from money," he explained gently. "She was working class, I'd say. Her hands showed signs of it, and her clothes were good but not quite good enough, and slightly out of style. She was putting on airs, trying to fit in here with this crowd, where she didn't really belong. And your daughter figured that out."

A sharp, bitter laugh erupted from his host. "Yes, I'm sure she did," he agreed. "Daphne has always been so concerned with style and fashion, she'd have spotted an imposter a mile away." He nodded brusquely. "So she saw that and figured Lisette must be a gold digger, here to find and marry some rich man for his fortune."

"Exactly. Which she may have been, at least in part." Davis felt for the other man as he continued, "and you were clearly the biggest potential catch, so your daughter didn't believe Lisette when she claimed she'd spurned your advances."

There was a hole in this theory, of course, and Trevor was not slow to catch it now that some of the shock had worn off. "But she put on my galoshes and my coat," he pointed out. "And used the side door instead of just crossing from the sitting room. That sounds like she'd already decided to kill Lisette and frame me for it."

"I think so, yes," Davis replied. "She probably saw her out there by the woods and decided to eliminate the threat and secure her inheritance at the same time." He watched the other man slump as he finally accepted the idea that his daughter, his eldest child, had not only killed someone in cold blood but had deliberately set him up to take the blame. "I'm sorry."

"Not as much as I am," Trevor mumbled, his words thick with grief. When he looked up at the detective again, his eyes brimmed with tears, but they were still sharp and clear. "Thank you, though. I am glad to know the truth, and not to go to prison for a crime I didn't commit." He wiped roughly at his eyes and cheeks with the back of one hand. "I'm just sorry an innocent girl is dead because of my daughter's greed and anger."

"Of course." Davis pushed away from the desk, ducked around to collect the boots with one hand, and then reclaim his hat from a nearby lamp with the other, and started toward the door. "Though if you want to thank someone, it should really be Winnie. It was she who thought to check your boots for perfume, and her performance that drew a confession from your daughter — and at great personal risk."

"Yes, you're right." Trevor rose and followed him. "I'll have to find her and thank her. I'm sure she's relieved, too, that her sister's killer was brought to justice."

"Odd thing, that," Davis commented, as he tugged the door open and twisted about to face his host a final time. "Lisette's body is still unclaimed and likely to remain so. My men did some checking and discovered that her real name was Lisa Burns and that she was from a small town a few hours away. She worked as a shop girl there — and she had no living relatives."

The older man gaped at him. "But Winnie, she said they were..."

"In all fairness, I'm not sure she ever did," the detective corrected, setting his hat on his head. "We all assumed that, and she never corrected us. I asked if they were sisters, but thinking back, all she answered was that Lisette was her responsibility." He grinned. "Another mystery, perhaps, but fortunately not one I need to solve." He offered his free hand. "Thank you for all your help and your co-operation, sir. We'll be in touch."

"Thank you." They shook, and Trevor watched Davis stride toward the front door and let himself out, a hush following him as he went and leaving the guests somber and subdued.

It seemed the party was finally over.

CHAPTER SEVENTEEN

Ignoring the whispers and the half-hearted attempts to draw him into conversation—no doubt to confirm the rumors and gain more concrete gossip first and commiserate a distant second—Trevor searched the house for his mysterious rescuer. He did not see Winnie anywhere, however—until he checked in the sunroom. It was still the dead of night and the room was pitch black and completely empty, but through its wall of windows, he spotted a flicker of someone moving across the lawn. Someone in soft gray.

Footsteps sounded behind him as he opened the glass doors, a man's and a woman's, but Trevor did not turn around even when the scents of tobacco, sherry, gin, and jasmine told him the newcomers were his two oldest friends. "Where are you off to, then?" Halsey asked, his voice gruff. "We were looking for you."

"I need to find that girl Winnie," he answered, stepping out onto the grass. "To thank her. I think I saw her go this way."

"Hm, yes, she did you a good turn, that girl," Sylvia agreed, the nearness of her voice confirming that she had just followed him out. "Perhaps she's paying respects to her sister one last time?"

"Not her sister," Trevor replied absently. He knew that wouldn't do, however, and so he quickly explained what the detective had revealed as he hurried across the lawn, his friends staying close at his side. He could just make out a pale shape that might be Winnie's face, though it was off to the side from where Lisette's body had been found. More aligned with that spot in the woods where he had seen the strange witness before.

That thought almost stopped him in his tracks, but his urgency propelled him forward even as his thoughts raced. Had it been Winnie he'd seen there before? If so, why hadn't she said anything? But if so, he was even more determined that she not escape again!

The three of them hurried across the grass, Halsey providing an arm to Sylvia, whose shoes were hardly suited to such an endeavor. But by the time they reached the woods, the girl had vanished!

"Hang about," Halsey instructed as Trevor peered anxiously into the deep shadows among the trees. "Ah, here, try this!" And a light blossomed behind him. His friend handed over a flashlight with a grin. "Thought, after the last time we were out here, it might be useful to keep on hand, in case we came back out after dark."

Trevor accepted it with a silent nod of thanks and shone the light into the trees. But no girl magically appeared. The light did reveal small footprints, however, the shape and the sharp impression at the rear suggesting they were from a lady's shoes. He stepped carefully among the branches and leaves and twigs, following the track—until it suddenly disappeared. Just as the witness's footprints had before!

"Ah." That was from Sylvia. "Of course." She rested a hand on her friend's arm. "I'm afraid you won't find her. Not now."

"What do you mean?" Trevor demanded. And on her other side, Halsey muttered, "Here we go again."

"Isn't it obvious?" she asked with a sniff. "You remember what I said before, about your witness?"

Trevor did indeed. How could he forget such insanity? "You claimed it was a creature—a Wink."

"*Wunk*," Sylvia corrected. "A Wunk, dear. And what did I say happened when they got spotted?"

"They dug a hole, leapt into it, and pulled it in after them." Trevor shook his head. "That's mad, Sylvie. I'm sorry, but it is."

"And yet—" she gestured at the ground before them, and the tracks that were there one second and completely gone the next. "How else do you explain it?"

"So what you're saying is… Winnie is also a Wunk?" Halsey asked. "So now we have two of them?"

"No, don't be daft," she corrected. "Just the one. Winnie *is* the Wunk—and your witness, too!"

"I don't think it was a girl I saw," Trevor pointed out. "I think it was a man. And the footprints match that."

"I told you, Wunks can change shape," she reminded them both as patiently as a mother correcting a well-meaning child's lessons.

"Clearly, the Wunk saw what happened, well enough to know it wasn't you that killed that poor girl. It was too shy to come forward but felt bad once it heard you were the suspect, so it took on a different form to help prove your innocence. Now its work is done and it's gone away again." She nudged Trevor with an elbow. "But I doubt it's gone far."

He studied his old friend. Sylvia was a kind soul and had a sharp eye and a sharper tongue and a steadfast, loyal heart. She also spoke nonsense occasionally, especially when she'd had a bit to drink, which was often. But right now, she seemed startlingly lucid and, if he ignored the utter impossibility of it all, what she said actually made sense. So, clearing his throat, he faced out into the woods and called out, "Winnie, I just wanted to thank you! Without you, I'd probably be in jail right now. You helped bring the real killer to justice." Then, embarrassed to be talking to the trees, he turned away.

"Well said," Sylvia agreed, patting him on the back. "Thank you, dear," she added over her shoulder, and Halsey nodded. Then the three of them headed back toward the house, where guests had begun to disperse now that the police had released them. Trevor was still wrestling with everything that had happened, but right now, with his two friends beside him, he felt he would get through it all. At least he still had them, and his health, and his home, and his son, who would need to be told everything. Soon. But for tonight, he decided that he needed a drink.

Behind them, under cover of the woods, a figure rose silently from out of the ground as if it had been poured upward, flowing into being and leaving unmarred dirt and grass at its feet. It peered out, watching the trio retreat, and nodded, content that justice had been served and peace restored — and that it had more than made up for any damage its own inconvenient disappearance earlier might have caused.

Still, perhaps it would be best to avoid parties for a while after this. Sometimes, they were more trouble than they were worth!

ABOUT THE AUTHOR

Aaron Rosenberg is the author of the best-selling DuckBob SF comedy series, the *Dread Remora* space-opera series, the Relicant Chronicles epic fantasy series, and—with David Niall Wilson—the O.C.L.T. occult thriller series. Aaron's tie-in work contains novels for *Star Trek, Warhammer, World of WarCraft, Stargate: Atlantis, Shadowrun, Eureka, Mutants & Masterminds,* and more. He has written children's books (including the original series STEM Squad and Pete and Penny's Pizza Puzzles, the award-winning *Bandslam: The Junior Novel,* and the #1 best-selling *42: The Jackie Robinson Story*), educational books on a variety of topics, and over seventy roleplaying games (such as the original games *Asylum, Spookshow,* and *Chosen,* work for White Wolf, Wizards of the Coast, Fantasy Flight, Pinnacle, and many others, and both the Origins Award-winning *Gamemastering Secrets* and the Gold ENnie-winning *Lure of the Lich Lord*). He is the co-creator of the ReDeus series, and a founding member of Crazy 8 Press. Aaron lives in New York with his family. You can follow him online at gryphonrose.com, on Facebook at facebook.com/gryphonrose, and on Twitter @gryphonrose.

artist's rendition of a Wunk

THE WUNK

ORIGINS: The Wunk is known first and foremost among the lumberjack communities of the United States. Due to the nature of the Wunk, it has not been proven if this creature exists, or if it evolved from the practice of hazing new immigrants

DESCRIPTION: A creature of the forest known for curiosity but also for being extremely shy. With no confirmed sightings, the creature's physical description has not been documented. While it watches those around it, when sighted, it retreats, not merely running away, but digging a hole in the ground to disappear into. Once in the hole, it pulls it in after itself, leaving no trace.

It is said to have the ability to transform into any creature and appear indistinguishable from the original, animal or human. By some accounts, the Wunk does not actually make use of this ability to escape detection, but it is also posited that if it did, how would the observer know? In either case, because of its particular nature, Wunk sightings are largely unreported and/or unrealized.

LIFE CYCLE: Unknown.

HISTORY: Earliest mentions of the Wunk appear in the late 19th to early 20th century.

POSSIBLE VARIATIONS:

SQUIDGICUM-SQUEE

ORIGINS: Also known among the lumberjack communities of the United States in the late 19th and early 20th centuries.

DESCRIPTION: The Squidgicum-Squee is accounted to be a big-mouthed creature with what appear to be trees growing out of its back. Rather than digging holes to hide in, this cryptid opens its mouth wide, breaths in deeply, and swallows itself whole.

There is no confirmation that these two creatures are related, but the similarities between them are noteworthy.

ABOUT THE ARTIST

Although Jason Whitley has worn many creative hats, he is at heart a traditional illustrator and painter. With author James Chambers, Jason collaborates and illustrates the sometimes-prose, sometimes graphic novel, *The Midnight Hour*, which is being collected into one volume by eSpec Books. His and Scott Eckelaert's newspaper comic strip, Sea Urchins, has been collected into four volumes. Along with eSpec Books' Systema Paradoxa series, Jason is working on a crime noir graphic novel. His portrait of Charlotte Hawkins Brown is on display in the Charlotte Hawkins Brown Museum.

CAPTURE THE CRYPTIDS!

Cryptid Crate is a monthly subscription box filled with various cryptozoology and paranormal themed items to wear, display and collect. Expect a carefully curated box filled with creeptastic pieces from indie makers and artisans pertaining to bigfoot, sasquatch, UFOs, ghosts, and other cryptid and mysterious creatures (apparel, decor, media, etc).

http://CryptidCrate.com